MARK TIDD

LECTOR HOUSE PUBLIC DOMAIN WORKS

This book is a result of an effort made by Lector House towards making a contribution to the preservation and repair of original classic literature. The original text is in the public domain in the United States of America, and possibly other countries depending upon their specific copyright laws.

In an attempt to preserve, improve and recreate the original content, certain conventional norms with regard to typographical mistakes, hyphenations, punctuations and/or other related subject matters, have been corrected upon our consideration. However, few such imperfections might not have been rectified as they were inherited and preserved from the original content to maintain the authenticity and construct, relevant to the work. We believe that this work holds historical, cultural and/or intellectual importance in the literary works community, therefore despite the oddities, we accounted the work for print as a part of our continuing effort towards preservation of literary work and our contribution towards the development of the society as a whole, driven by our beliefs.

We are grateful to our readers for putting their faith in us and accepting our imperfections with regard to preservation of the historical content. We shall strive hard to meet up to the expectations to improve further to provide an enriching reading experience.

Though, we conduct extensive research in ascertaining the status of copyright before redeveloping a version of the content, in rare cases, a classic work might be incorrectly marked as not-in-copyright. In such cases, if you are the copyright holder, then kindly contact us or write to us, and we shall get back to you with an immediate course of action.

HAPPY READING!

MARK TIDD

CLARENCE BUDINGTON KELLAND

ISBN: 978-93-5342-546-3

First Published: -

LECTOR HOUSE LLP
E-MAIL: lectorpublishing@gmail.com

"GO FOR BATTEN. I'M RIGHT HERE, AND I'LL LOOK AFTER BILL"

MARK TIDD

HIS ADVENTURES AND STRATEGIES

BY

CLARENCE B. KELLAND

ILLUSTRATED BY
W. W. CLARKE

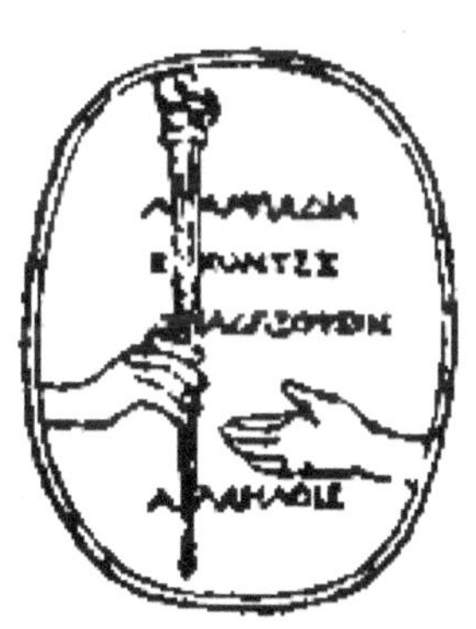

Books by

CLARENCE BUDINGTON KELLAND

Mark Tidd in Egypt
Mark Tidd in Italy
Mark Tidd
Mark Tidd in the Backwoods
Mark Tidd in Business
Mark Tidd's Citadel
Mark Tidd, Editor
Mark Tidd, Manufacturer
Catty Atkins, Bandmaster
Catty Atkins
Catty Atkins, Riverman
Catty Atkins, Sailorman
Catty Atkins, Financier

CONTENTS

LIST OF ILLUSTRATIONS

MARK TIDD

CHAPTER I

My name is Martin—James Briggs Martin—but almost everybody calls me Tallow, because once when I was younger I saw old Uncle Ike Bond rubbing tallow on his boots to shine them, and then hurried home and fixed mine up with the stub of a candle and went to school. I guess it couldn't have smelled very good, for everybody seemed to notice it, even teacher, and she asked me what in the world I'd been getting into. After that all the boys called me Tallow, and always will, I guess.

I tell you about me first only because I'm writing this account of what happened. Mark Tidd is really the fellow I'm writing about, and Mark's father and mother, and the engine Mr. Tidd was inventing out in his barn, and some other folks who will be told about in their places. I helped some; so did Plunk Smalley and Binney Jenks, but Mark Tidd did most of it. Mark Tidd sounds like a short name, doesn't it? But it isn't short at all, for it's merely what's left of Marcus Aurelius Fortunatus Tidd, which was what he was christened, mostly out of Gibbon's Decline and Fall of the Roman Empire, a big book that Mr. Tidd was so fond of reading that he never read much of anything else except the papers.

Mark Tidd was the last of us four boys to move to Wicksville. I was born there, and so was Plunk Smalley, but Binney Jenks moved over from Sunfield when he was five. Mark he didn't come to town until a little over a year ago, and Plunk and me saw him get off the train at the depot. I guess the car must have been glad when he did get off, for he looked like he almost filled it up. Yes, sir, when he came out of the door he had to squeeze to get through. He was the fattest boy I ever saw, or ever expect to see, and the funniest-looking. His head was round and 'most as big as a pretty good-sized pumpkin, and his cheeks were so fat they almost covered up his eyes. The rest of him was as round as his face, and Plunk said one of his legs was as big as all six of Plunk's and Binney's and mine put together. I guess it was bigger. When Plunk and me saw him we just rolled over and kicked up our legs and hollered.

"I hope he's goin' to live in Wicksville," says Plunk, "'cause we won't care then if a circus never comes."

A fat boy like that is a good thing to have in a town, so when things sort of slow down you can always go and have fun with him. At any rate, that was what we thought then. It seemed to us that Marcus Aurelius Fortunatus Tidd was a ready-made joke put right into our hands for us to fool with, but afterward we changed our minds considerable.

Mark's father and mother got off the train after him, and his father said something to him we couldn't hear. Mark waddled across the platform to where Uncle Ike Bond's bus stood waiting, and Plunk and me listened to hear what he would say.

"D-d-do you c-carry p-p-p-passengers in that b-bus?" Yes, sir, he said it just like that!

Well, Plunk he looked at me and I looked at him, and he soaked me in the ribs and I smashed his hat down over his eyes, we were so tickled. If we had been going to plan a funny kid we couldn't have done half so well. We'd have forgot something sure. But nothing was forgot in Mark Tidd, even to the stutter.

Old Uncle Ike looked down off his seat at Mark, and his eyes popped out like he couldn't believe what they saw. He waited a minute before he said anything, sort of planning in his mind what he was going to say, I guess. That was a way Uncle Ike had, and then he usually said something queer. This time he says:

"Passengers? What? Me carry passengers? No. I've just got this bus backed up here to stiddy the depot platform. The railroad comp'ny pays me to do it."

Mark Tidd he looked solemn at Uncle Ike, and Uncle Ike looked solemn at him. Then Mark says, respectful and not impertinent:

"If I was to sit here and hold down the p-p-platform could you drive my folks? I could keep it from m-m-movin' much."

Uncle Ike blinked. "Son," says he, "climb aboard, if this here rattletrap looks safe to you, and fetch along your folks. We'll leave the platform stand without hitchin' for wunst."

At that me and Plunk turned to look at the fat boy's father and mother. Mr. Tidd was a long man, upward of six foot, I guess, and not very wide. His shoulders kind of sloped like his head was too heavy for them, and his head was so big that it was no wonder. His hair was getting gray in front of his ears where it showed under his hat, and he had blue eyes and thin cheeks and a sort of far-off, pleasant expression, like he was thinking of something nice a long ways away. He was leaning against a corner of the station reading out of a big book and paying no attention to anybody. Afterward I found out the book was Gibbon's Decline and Fall, and that he always carried it around with him to read in a little when he got a spare minute.

Mrs. Tidd wasn't that kind of person at all. As soon as Plunk and me looked at her we knew she could make bully pies, and wouldn't get mad if her fat boy was to sneak into the pantry and cut a slice out of one of them in the middle of the afternoon. You could tell she was patient and good-natured, but, all the same, she wasn't the kind you could fool. If you came home with your hair wet it wouldn't do any good to tell her somebody threw a pail of water on it. She was looking around to see what she could see, and I bet she didn't miss much.

The fat boy he motioned to her to come to the bus, and she spoke to her husband. He looked up sort of vague, nodded his head, and came poking across the platform, holding his book in front of him and reading away as though he hadn't a minute to spare, and clean forgot all about the valise he'd set down beside him.

"Jeffrey," says Mrs. Tidd, "you've forgot your satchel."

He shut his book, but kept his finger in the place, and looked all around him. Pretty soon he saw the satchel and nodded his head at it. "So I have," he says, "so I have," and went back to get it.

Then all of them got into Uncle Ike's bus, and he stirred up his horses who had been standing 'most asleep, with heads drooping, and they went rattling and banging up the street. When Uncle Ike's bus got started you could hear it half a mile. I guess it was all loose, for it sounded like a hail-storm beating down on a tin roof.

"Wonder where they're goin'?" says Plunk.

"You got to do more'n wonder if you're goin' to find out," I says, and started trotting after the bus. It wasn't hard to keep it in sight, because Uncle Ike's horses got tired every little while and came to a walk.

They stopped at the old Juniper house that had been standing vacant for six months, ever since old man Juniper went to Chicago to live with his daughter Susy's oldest girl that had married a man with a hardware store there. The yard was full of boxes and packing-cases and furniture all done up with burlap and rope.

"They're goin' to live here," Plunk yells; and I was as glad as he was. The benefits of having a stuttering fat boy living near you aren't to be sneezed at by anybody.

We found a shady place across the street and watched to see what would happen. It's always interesting to watch other folks work, especially if what they're doing is hard work, and I guess carrying furniture and trunks and boxes is about as hard as anything.

Mrs. Tidd was ready for work before anybody else. She came to the door with a big apron on and a cloth tied around her hair, and the way she sailed into things was a caution. It seemed like she jumped right into the middle of that mess, and in a minute things were flying. Mr. Tidd came next with his book under his arm and stood in the stoop looking sort of puzzled. Mrs. Tidd straightened up, and then sat down on a packing-box.

"Jeffrey Tidd," she said, not sharp and angry, but kind of patient and rebuking, "go right back into the house and take those clothes off. I knew if I didn't stay right by you you'd get mixed up somehow. Will you tell me why in the world you changed from your second-best clothes to that Sunday black suit to move furniture?"

Mr. Tidd he looked pretty foolish and felt of his pants as though he couldn't believe they were his best ones.

"That does beat all," he said. "It does beat all creation, Libby. I wonder how these clothes come to be on me?"

"If you didn't have 'em on under your others, which ain't impossible, you must have changed into 'em."

"My best suit!" he said to himself, shaking his head like you've seen the elephant do at the circus, first to one side and then to the other. "My best clothes!"

"Maybe I'd better come along and see you get into the right ones this time," Mrs. Tidd suggested.

"I guess you don't need to, Libby. I'll take these off and hang 'em in the closet, and I'll hang my second-best ones up, too. Then I'll put on what's left. That way I can't go wrong." He went off into the house, and Mrs. Tidd flew at the piles of stuff again.

Pretty soon the fat boy came around the side of the house with a quarter of a cherry pie in his hand and the juice dripping down faster than he could suck it off.

"Marcus," his mother called, "take holt of this bundle of bed-slats and carry 'em up to the front room."

Mark he grabbed them with one hand and hunched them up under his arm so that one end dragged on the ground, walking off slow and eating pie as he went. It took him quite a while to get back. I could see him look across the street at Plunk and me as he came down the steps. He stopped a minute, sort of thinking.

After a while Mr. Tidd came back again.

"Put the Decline and Fall down somewheres so you can use both hands, Jeffrey," his wife says. And he did it as meek and obedient as could be. Between them they carried a hair-cloth sofa in after she had told Mark to fetch along some medium-sized boxes.

Mark stooped over one, and we could hear him grunt.

"Hello, Skinny," Plunk yells. "Git your back into it and h'ist. That's the way to lift."

The fat boy straightened up and looked at us quite a while. Then he sat down on the box and called, "I bet the two of you can't l-l-lift it."

"I'll bet," says Plunk, "we kin lift it. I'll bet we kin carry it from here to the standpipe and back without lettin' her down wunst."

"Braggin' don't carry no b-boxes."

The way he said it sort of made me mad. "Come on, Plunk," I says; "lets show this here hippopotamus whether we kin carry it or not." And we went running across the street.

"Where d'you want it put?" I says.

"No use you tryin'. You couldn't g-git it up."

"Git holt," I says to Plunk. "Now, Mister What's-your-name, where's it go?"

"Up-stairs in the hall; but you b-b-better not try. It's too heavy for you."

Plunk and me took that box up-stairs a-flying and ran down again.

"There," I says. "Now kin we carry it?"

He stuck up what there was to his nose. "One ain't nothin'. I carried the hull twelve out when we was movin' in fifteen mum-minutes."

"If you did," I says, "Plunk and me can carry 'em in in twelve."

He just laughed.

"Doggone it," I says, "we'll show you, you're so smart."

"Can't d-d-do it."

"You ain't the only kid that can carry things," Plunk says, with a scowl.

Mark he pulled out a little silver watch and held it in his hand. "Twelve m-minutes, was it? Can't do it. I'll keep time."

Well, Plunk and me went at those boxes like sixty, and the way we ran them up-stairs was a terror to cats. When the last one was up we were panting and sweating and most tuckered out. Mark looked off his watch when we came out with a sort of surprised expression. "You kids is stronger than I figgered. You did it in eleven minutes and a half."

"Sure," I says.

"But them boxes wasn't very heavy. You can't carry that big box, by j-jimminy!"

Plunk and me was good and mad, and if anybody'd seen the way we hustled that big box in they wouldn't have believed their eyes.

"That's perty good," says Mark. "Wouldn't thought it of you kids. Must be stronger here in Wicksville than over to Peckstown where I come from." He stopped a minute. "I can't lift that big rockin'-c-c-chair myself."

"Huh!" snorted Plunk. "That's a easy one." And in we wrastled with the chair.

We weren't going to have any strange kid think we weren't up to all he was, so we stayed right there all the afternoon, and I guess we proved pretty conclusively we could carry. And that wasn't all: we proved we could last. I bet we carried two-thirds of the Tidds' furniture in. When it was all done we sat down on the fence to pant and rest. Mark's mother called him.

"I got to go to s-s-s-supper," he says. "Come again when you feel s-s-strong." And then he went into the house.

Plunk and me sat still quite a while. I began to think about it and think about it, and I could see Plunk was thinking, too. In about fifteen minutes I looked over at him and he looked over at me.

PLUNK AND ME WAS GOOD AND MAD

"How many things did that fat kid carry in?" I says.

"I didn't see him carry anythin'."

"Neither did I."

We thought quite a spell more. Then I said to Plunk, "I guess maybe we better not do too much braggin' about how much an' how long we kin carry."

He grinned kind of sickly. "This here Mark Tidd," he says, "ain't nobody's fool—leastways, not on Mondays, which is to-day."

When we got better acquainted with Mark Tidd he read a book called Tom Sawyer to us. I guess he got his idea of making us work out of that; he was always taking schemes out of books.

CHAPTER II

Mrs. Tidd was just the kind of person I thought she would be. She cooked lots of things and cooked them good; and, no matter how often Mark wanted to eat, she never said a word. Plunk and Binney Jenks and me got to going there a lot, and there was always cookies and pie and things. Of course, we didn't go specially to eat, but knowing we'd get something wasn't any drawback. I liked Mrs. Tidd, and sort of admired her, too. She was always working at something and managing things and keeping track of Mr. Tidd and Mark. I never heard her complain, and I don't remember ever seeing her sit down except in the cool of the evening after supper.

I don't want you to get the idea that Mr. Tidd was lazy or shiftless, because he wasn't. He was just queer, and his memory was as long as a piece of string, which is the way we have in Wicksville of saying there was no knowing just how long it really was. Lots of times I've seen Mr. Tidd start out to do a job of work and forget all about it before he got a chance to commence. He was sure to forget if Mrs. Tidd didn't take the *Decline and Fall* away from him before he went out of the door. Even that didn't make it certain, because something to think about might pop into his head all of a sudden, and if it did he had to sit down and think about it then and there. He was a machinist complicated by inventions. Every time he saw you doing anything he'd stop right there and invent a better way for you to do it; and mostly the new ways he invented wouldn't work.

It was an invention that had brought all the Tidds to Wicksville. Mark told us about it. It seems like Mr. Tidd had been inventing a new kind of machine or engine or something that he called a turbine. He'd been working on it a long time, making pictures of it and figuring it out in his head, but he never had a chance to get right down to business and actually *invent* it till a little while before they came to our town. Then an aunt of his up and died and left him some money. He quit his job right off and came to Wicksville, where it was quiet and cheap, to finish up doing the inventing. When he got it done he wouldn't need a job any more because it would make him rich. We used to go out in the barn, where he was tinkering away, and watch him for hours at a time, and he never paid any more attention to us than as if we weren't there at all. But he was careful about other folks and wouldn't let them step a foot inside of the door. He was afraid somebody would see what he was up to and go do it first, which would have been a mean trick.

Mr. Tidd wasn't what you call *suspicious*; he wasn't always expecting somebody that he knew to do something to his engine, and I guess any man that had wanted to could have got into the workshop and looked it all over to his heart's content by talking to Mr. Tidd for an hour or so and listening to him tell about the

Roman Empire, and how it split down the middle and went all to smash. He was the kind-heartedest man in the world, I guess, and never could see any bad in any one—not in any one he really saw. He had a sort of far-away idea that there was bad folks, and that some of them might want to steal his invention, but if he had seen a man crawling through a window of the barn he'd have found some excuse for him. Anybody could fool him—that is, they could have if Mrs. Tidd hadn't been there; but she kept her eye on him pretty close and saw to it he didn't let any strangers come fooling around. If everybody had been as careful as she was this story wouldn't have happened.

The real beginning of things didn't look like anything important at all. It happened one afternoon when Mark Tidd and Plunk and Binney and me were hanging around the depot platform waiting for the train to come in. We didn't expect anybody we knew to come, and there wasn't any reason for our being there except that there wasn't any reason for our being anywhere else. Plunk and I sat on one of those baggage-trucks that run along straight for a while and then turn up a hill at the end; Binney sat on a trunk; and Mark was on the platform, because that was the safest place for him and wouldn't break down. It was hot and sleepy, and we wished we were somewheres else or that something exciting would happen. It didn't, so we just sat there and talked, and finally we got to talking about Mr. Tidd's engine. We'd seen him tinkering around it, and he'd told us about it, so we were interested.

"Wouldn't it be great," says Binney, "if it worked when he got it done! Us fellers could say all the rest of our lives that we knew intimate a inventor that was as big as Edison."

We never had thought about that part of it before; but what Binney said was so, and we got more anxious than ever for things to turn out right.

"If it does," says Plunk, "Mark'll be rich, and maybe live to the hotel. Think of bein' able to spend a dollar 'n' a half every day for nothin' but meals and a place to sleep."

Mark he didn't say anything, because he was drowsy and his head was nodding.

"Mr. Tidd says it'll reverlutionize the world," Binney put in. "He says if them Romans had had one of his gas-turbines the empire never'd have fell."

"If it goes, nothin' else'll be used to run automobiles. If Mr. Tidd sold a engine for ev'ry automobile in the United States I guess he could afford livin' to the hotel. I'll bet he could own a automobile himself."

"And they'll use 'em in fact'ries and steamboats, 'cause they kin be run with steam same as with gasolene."

"And won't be more'n a twentieth as big as engines is now."

We kept on talking and describing what we thought Mr. Tidd's turbine would do and guessing how long it would be before he was ready to try it to see if it went. We was so interested we never noticed a man sitting a little ways off on a trunk. Pretty soon we did notice him, though, for he got up deliberate like and stretched himself and looked around as if he didn't see anything, including us. Then his eyes lit on Mark, and he kind of grinned. He lighted a cigar and came walking over toward us.

"How about this train?" he asks, like he wasn't much interested but wanted to talk to pass away the time. "Is it generally much behind?"

"Not much," I says. "I ain't known it to be over a hour late for two weeks."

"Live here?" he asks, with another grin.

I nodded, but didn't say anything out loud.

"Pretty quiet place for boys, isn't it?"

"It ain't what most folks'd call excitin'."

After a minute he says: "I used to live in a little town like this when I was a boy, and I remember there wasn't very much to do. I used to hang around the carpenter shop watching the carpenters work, and around the machine shop seeing how the machinists did things. It was pretty interesting. I suppose you do the same here."

"We-ell, it ain't exactly a machine shop we hang around."

"Oh," he says, "what is it?"

"It's a—a—"

Just then Mark seemed to wake up sudden He grunted and interrupted what I was going to say, and then did the saying himself. "It's a b-barn," he says.

"Oh," says the man, "a barn? What do you watch in the barn? The horses?"

"No. Ain't no h-h-horses." Then he half shut his eyes like he was going to take another nap.

The man didn't say anything for a spell. "I was always interested in machines when I was a boy," he says, at last. "Any kind of a machine or engine got me all excited. But we didn't have as fine machines then as you do now. They're making improvements and inventing new things every day. Some day they're going to invent something to make locomotives better—something along the turbine line, I expect. Know what a turbine is?"

I was just going to say yes, when Mark woke up again. "Yes," he says, "a t-t-turbine is a climbin' vine that grows over p-porches."

The man kind of strangled and looked away. "No," he says in a minute, "I guess you got it mixed up with woodbine."

"Maybe so," says Mark.

We heard the engine whistle, and the man hurried off to see about his baggage. The train pulled in and pulled out again and left us sitting on the platform wondering what to do next. Mark stood up slow and tired and yawned till it seemed like his head would come off.

"Fellers," says he, "you gabble like a lot of geese. Looked like that man was more'n ord'nary interested in engines."

"'Spose he heard what we was talking about?"

Mark looked at me disgusted. "Tallow," says he, "don't go layin' down in no pastures, 'cause a muley cow 'thout horns'll come and chaw a hunk out of your p-p-pants."

"I guess I ain't so green," I told him, but he only grinned.

"Let's go swimmin'," says Binney.

Mark shook his head and looked solemn. "Go ahead if you want to. No swimmin' for me; it's Friday, and I stepped on a spider this mornin'."

Plunk busted out laughing. "Haw," he says, "believin' in signs. I ain't superstitious."

Mark looked at him and blinked. "I ain't superstitious, but I don't b'lieve in takin' extra chances. Probably there ain't nothin' in it, but you can't never tell."

That illustrates better than I can tell what kind of a fellow Mark Tidd was—cautious, looking on all sides of a thing he was thinking of doing, always trying to figure plans out ahead so nothing disagreeable could happen. I don't want you to think he was a coward, because he wasn't, but he never ran his head into trouble that could be dodged ahead of time.

We all started for the river, because it would be cooler there even if we didn't go in, but on the way Mark found a four-leaf clover, and a white cat ran across the road in front of us, so he figured it out that if there *was* any bad luck about Friday and killing a spider those two good-luck signs had knocked the spots off it.

CHAPTER III

Mark Tidd wasn't given much to exercise, but that isn't saying he couldn't stir around spry if there was some good reason. He never wanted to play baseball or tag or anything where you had to run, and usually when a game was going on he'd be lying under a tree reading a book. He said it was a lot easier reading about a game than playing it, and more interesting than watching the kind we played. He read a good deal, anyhow, mostly, I guess, because you can sit so still to do it, and rest at the same time if you want to; and it was surprising the things he got to know about that were useful to us. Seemed like almost everything we wanted to do Mark would have read about some better way of doing it, and that's how we came to get up the K. K. K., which stands for Ku Klux Klan.

We were all sitting in Tidd's yard where the shade of the barn fell, and nobody had said anything for quite a spell. I was beginning to want to do something, and it was easy to see that Plunk and Binney were wriggling around uneasy like; but Mark he lay with his little eyes shut tight, looking as peaceful and satisfied as a turtle on a log. All of a sudden the idea popped into my head, and I yelled right out, "Let's git up a secret society."

Mark opened one eye and sort of blinked at me, and Plunk and Binney sat up straight.

"What'll we call it?" Binney wanted to know.

"Who'll be officers?" Plunk asked.

"I dunno," I says, sharp like, because they seemed to think I ought to have the whole thing planned out for them to do without their lifting a hand.

Mark rubbed his eyes and rolled over on his side. "What's the main thing about a s-secret society?" he asks.

"Payin' dues," I says, quick.

"Havin' somethin' to eat," Binney guessed.

"Naw," Mark grunts, contemptuous. "The main thing about a secret society is the s-s-secret."

We could see in a minute that he was right about that.

"So," he went on, "if we're goin' to have a secret society the first thing is to git a s-s-secret to have."

"I don't know no secret," Binney said, shaking his head hard.

"Nor me," said Plunk.

I thought a minute, because I knew a couple of secrets, but they were secrets I didn't calculate to tell anybody, least of all Mark and Plunk and Binney; so I just shook my head, too.

"We'll make a secret," Mark told us.

"How?" I wanted to know, because I didn't see how you could go to work to make a secret, but I might have known Mark would find a way.

"Did you ever hear of the K-k-k-ku K-k-k-klux K-k-k-klan?"

"What?" I asked.

He said it over again.

"I didn't git it that time," I told him. "Sounds like a tongue-tied hen tryin' to cackle."

Mark sort of scowled at me and did it all over, but not one of us could make a thing of it.

"Write it," I said; "that's the only way we'll ever git it."

At first he wasn't going to do it, but we argued with him that it wasn't any use spoiling a good thing like a secret society just because he couldn't mention plain a name he wanted to tell us; so at last he wrote it down on a piece of paper. What he wrote was Ku Klux Klan.

"It don't make no sense," Binney said. "What language is it, anyhow? Dutch?"

"It ain't no language. It's a name."

"Oh."

"Of the most p-p-powerful secret society that ever was."

"I reckon it was over in Russia or somewheres. It sounds like it."

"It was right here in the United States."

"Hum," I said, because that name didn't sound a bit like the United States to me.

"It was after the war."

"The Spanish War?"

"No. The North and South war."

"Oh.... That one. What was it for?"

"For protection. They went ridin' around at night rightin' wrongs and scarin' folks and runnin' things in general. They wore white sheets over their heads."

"Gee. Honest?"

"It's in the histories."

"And it was secret?"

"The most secret thing ever was. Even men in it didn't know who one another was."

"Let's have one," Plunk yelled, squirming around like he was sitting on an ant's nest. "I kin git a sheet."

"Who's goin' to b'long?" I said; and then we all looked at one another.

"Nobody but us four," Binney whispers, because he's beginning to feel secret already. There wasn't any argument to that, so we agreed to be a Ku Klux Klan, and to have our secret meeting-place in a little cave up across from the island where the swimming-hole was. It wasn't much of a cave. Just a little round room dug out of the hill by somebody a long time ago. I couldn't stand up straight in it, and when we four was all inside there wasn't much room left—not with Mark Tidd taking up the space he did.

Well, each of us got a sheet and hid it there, and we kept potatoes to bake and an old frying-pan and a kettle and other things like that in case of emergency, for there was no knowing what might come up with an organization like ours, and we knew we had to be ready. Mark made up passwords and grips and secret signs; and we had an alphabet all of our own that we could write letters to one another in, which was fine, even though there never seemed to be anything very secret to write. But there come to be later on, and there was a time when we was glad of the cave and the potatoes and the frying-pan. But that wasn't until the next spring, and lots of things happened before then.

I guess maybe it was a month after we organized the Klan when the stranger came to town. We were cooking dinner up at the cave that day—a black bass, four perch, and a couple of blue-gills, with baked potatoes—and we were just scouring the dishes with sand when we looked down and saw Uncle Ike Bond come ambling along the river. Uncle Ike drove the bus when it was necessary and fished the rest of the time, which was most of the time; and he caught fish, too; lots of them. I guess he got a good many on night lines.

Binney Jenks yelled down at Uncle Ike, and he looked up to see who it was. When he recognized Mark Tidd he sat down sort of tired on a log and motioned for us to come. He was a great friend of Mark's since the day the Tidds moved to town; and he let on to folks that Mark was the smartest boy in Wicksville, which I wouldn't be surprised if he was.

We all went down the hill, three of us running, and Mark panting along behind and puffing and snorting.

"Expectin' any visitors?" Uncle Ike asked of Mark.

"No," said Mark, and sat down.

"Um!" grunted Uncle Ike.

He pulled out his pipe and fussed at it with his jack-knife before he filled it and lighted up. "Looks kinder like you was goin' to have some," he said.

Mark didn't answer anything or ask questions, because if you do Uncle Ike is apt to shut up like a clam and not tell you another thing. He waited, knowing Ike'd tell on if there was anything to say. The old man puffed away for a spell and then asked:

"Father's makin' some sort of a whirligig, ain't he?"

"Yes. He's inventin' a e-e-engine."

"Um!" grunted Uncle Ike. "Calc'late it's wuth anythin'?"

Mark nodded yes.

"Feller come in on the mornin' train that seemed tolerable int'rested in sich whirligigs," said Uncle Ike. "He allowed to set onto the seat with me and asked was I acquainted in town—me! Asked was I acquainted in town!" It was hard for me to tell whether this made Uncle Ike mad or tickled him. He was that way, and you never could make him out. Sometimes when he was maddest he looked most tickled, and when he was most tickled he looked maddest.

"I allowed as how I knowed a few of the citizens by sight and more'n a dozen to speak to," Uncle Ike went on, "and then he up and begun wantin' to know. When folks gits to the wantin'-to-know stage on short acquaintance I git to the don't-want-to-tell stage, and Mister Man didn't collect no amazin' store of knowledge, not while he was a-ridin' on *my* bus."

He stopped talking and looked at Mark, and Mark looked at him. Then Uncle Ike winked at Mark. "If I was a smart boy," he said, "and a stranger feller come to town snoopin' around and askin' questions about whirligigs, I'd sorter look into it, I would. And if that stranger feller was askin' about the i-dentical kind of a whirligig my father was makin' in the barn and calc'latin' to git rich out of I'd look into it perty close. And if my father was one of these here inventor fellers that forgits their own names and would trust a cow to walk through a cornfield I'd be perty sharp and plannin' and keep my eye peeled. That's what I'd do, and I ain't drove a bus these twenty years for nothin', neither. The place to git eddicated," he said, "is on top of a bus. There ain't nothin' like it. There's where you see folks goin' away and comin' home, and there's where you see strangers and actors and travelin'-men, and everybody that walks the face of the earth. Colleges is all right, maybe, for readin' and writin', but when it comes to knowin' who you kin depend on and who you got to look out for the bus is the place."

"Did he ask about f-f-father?" Mark wanted to know.

"He didn't mention him by name," said Uncle Ike, grinning. "But he says to me, says he, 'This is a nice town,' says he, 'and a town that looks as if there was smart folks in it. It's lettle towns like this,' he says, 'that inventors and other great men comes from,' says he. 'Have you got any inventors here?' he asks.

"'There's Pete Biggs,' I says. 'He's up and invented a way to live without workin'.'

"'Is that all?' he asks, kind of disappointed.

"'Wa-al,' I says, like I was tryin' hard to remember, 'I *did* hear that Slim Peters invented some kind of a new front gate that would keep itself shut. But 'twan't no go,' I says, ''cause Slim he had to chop down the gate with a ax,' I says, 'the first time he wanted to go through it. It was a fine gate to stay shut,' I says, 'but it wa'n't no good at all to come open.'

"'Ain't there anybody here tryin' to make an engine?' he put in.

"'Engine?' says I. 'Engines is already invented, ain't they? What's the use inventin' when some other feller's done it first?'

"'I mean a new kind of an engine,' he says, 'a kind they call a turbine?'

"'Oh,' says I. 'I ain't met up with no engines like that, not in Wicksville. We ain't much on fancy names here, and I guess if a Wicksville feller had invented anythin' he wouldn't have named it that—he'd 'a' called it a engine right out.'

"'Umph!' says the feller, like he was mad, and then got out at the hotel. I stopped long enough to see him talkin' with Bert Sawyer, so it's likely he knowed all Bert did inside of ten minutes. And that's all there was to it." He looked at Mark with his eyes twinkling.

Mark got up kind of slow, blinking his eyes and looking back at Uncle Ike.

"I guess I'll go home," he said.

Uncle Ike slapped his knee and laughed a rattling kind of laugh way down in his throat. "There," he whispered, like he was talking confidential to Binney and Plunk and me, "what'd I tell you? Hey? What'd I tell you? Don't take him long to make up his mind, eh? Quicker'n a flash; slicker'n greased lightnin'!"

We went off up the hill after Mark, leaving Uncle Ike sitting on the log laughing to himself and slapping his leg every minute or so. He sat there till we were out of sight.

CHAPTER IV

Mark was pretty quiet walking along, thinking hard what to do, or whether he had better do anything; but finally he seemed to make up his mind and hurried off faster than I ever saw him walk before. And it was a warm day, too. We turned into his yard, and as we went through the gate he jerked his thumb toward the back yard.

"You w-w-wait there," he stuttered. "I may want you." Then he went in the front door.

As we walked by we looked through the window and saw the stranger sitting in the parlor talking to Mr. Tidd, and he was nodding and smiling and being very polite; or, anyhow, it seemed that way to me. I always was sort of curious, so I stopped close to the window and listened, while Plunk and Binney went on around the house. I guess it isn't very nice to listen that way, but I never thought of that until it was all over.

Mr. Tidd was talking.

"Yes, sir," he was saying, "the world don't hold another book like this. The title says it's *The Decline and Fall of the Roman Empire*, but it's about more than that. Why, it's about everything. It don't matter what happens, you can find the answer to it in Gibbon.... Yes, sir, *The Decline and Fall* is the greatest book of 'em all."

"I agree with you entirely, Mr. Tidd, entirely. It has been some time since I read the book, sir, but I have been promising myself that pleasure—and profit— for several months. I shall read it again, sir, as soon as I get home."

"You will never regret it," said Mr. Tidd, and patted the book in his lap.

Somehow the stranger's face seemed familiar to me, but for a while I couldn't place him. Then all of a sudden it came to me: he was the man we saw on the depot platform who asked about turbines. I almost yelled out loud to Mark.

I listened again and heard the stranger say:

"I'm in the engineering business, Mr. Tidd, and that's why I came to see you. I heard you were working on some sort of a machine, and, as my company always wants to keep in touch with the latest developments of mechanics and engineering, I dropped in to have a chat with you."

"Yes, yes," said Mr. Tidd; but it was plain he was thinking about something else.

"It happens often," said the stranger, "that men like yourself, who have valuable ideas, lack the money to carry them out. Very frequently my company, if the idea seems all right, advances the money to carry on experiments."

"Money," said Mr. Tidd, vaguely. "Oh yes, money. I don't need money. No. I have all the money I need."

The stranger looked disappointed, but he didn't say anything about it.

"You're fortunate," he told Mr. Tidd, "but maybe there's something else I could do for you."

"Not as I know of. Don't seem like I needed a thing, but I'm much obliged, much obliged."

"What is the nature of the work you are doing?" asked the man. I didn't think he liked to come right out with the question that way, but probably he couldn't invent any other way to get at it.

"It's a turbine," said Mr. Tidd, right off, and his eyes began to shine. "It's a practical turbine for locomotives and automobiles and power-plants and what not. Why, sir, this engine of mine will stand on a base no bigger than a cook-stove and develop two hundred horse-power; and it will be reversible. I have a new principle, sir, for the application of steam; a new principle, it is—" He stopped suddenly, shook his head, and said, with a patient sort of smile, "My folks don't like to have me talk too much about it."

"Of course," agreed the stranger, who had been leaning forward and edging farther toward the front of his chair, with interest. "Of course. It is never wise to discuss such things too freely. How far has your work progressed?"

"Not far, not far. In the experimental stages. I have something to show for my work—nothing to boast of, but enough. Enough to make me sure."

"I should be very interested to look over your workshop," suggested the stranger. "I always like to see how a thorough machinist has things arranged."

At that I ducked and ran around the house, and just a moment later Mark came tiptoeing out of the kitchen door. He held up his finger for us to be still and then motioned for us to follow him to the barn.

In the barn he grabbed up a lot of drawings and stuffed them into my hands.

"Here. Take these and hide back of the f-f-fence."

Then he gave Binney and Plunk some funny-looking pieces of steel to carry, and snatched some other things himself, and we all sneaked out through the back gate and crouched down behind the fence out of sight.

"Father's goin' to s-show him the shop," whispered Mark. "I guess the feller was fixin' to git a squint at these things. If he was it's all right, and if he wasn't no harm's done."

In about two shakes of a lamb's tail Mr. Tidd and the stranger came out of the shop and went inside. We had our ears to the wall and could hear how Mr. Tidd was being taffied by the man, and we could tell by the way he answered back that he was getting to like the stranger more and more every minute. Butter wouldn't melt in that man's mouth. He was as full of compliments as an old grist-mill is of rats.

After a while we heard Mr. Tidd say:

"I dunno's there'd be any objection to your lookin' at my drawin's and patterns and stuff. 'Twon't do no harm, I calc'late."

The man didn't say anything, and pretended he wasn't paying attention. We could hear Mr. Tidd moving around, and then he stopped still, and I knew he was scratching his head, though I couldn't see him, because he always scratches his head when he can't figure out just what's going on.

"I swan," he said, kind of vague and wondering, "I'd 'a' bet I left them things right here; I'd 'a' bet a cookie. But they ain't here—not a sign of 'em. Now, ain't that the beatenist? I must 'a' carted 'em off some place without thinkin'. Um! Hum!... Where'n tunket could it 'a' been?"

"What seems to be the matter?" asked the stranger, and his voice sounded anxious to me. It did to Mark, too, because he nudged me.

"I've up and mislaid my drawin's and things," said Mr. Tidd, sounding like he was apologizing. "Ain't that the dumbest thing! I'm always a-layin' things around and forgettin' 'em."

"Surely they must be in the shop some place," suggested the stranger.

Again we could hear Mr. Tidd rummaging around, but it wasn't any use. "No," he said, "no, they ain't here. I wonder if I could 'a' left 'em down to the grocery."

"What would you be doing with them at the grocery?"

"Nothin' that I know of, but I might have tucked 'em under my arm and gone just the same. Like's not I did. Wa-all, I'm sorry I can't show 'em to you, but maybe they'll turn up to-morrow."

"I've got to leave on the late train," said the stranger.

"Too bad," said Mr. Tidd, his mind still wondering where his things were. "Too bad." And with that he forgot all about the stranger and went out of the barn and off up the street talking to himself and scratching his head. The stranger looked after him and bit his lips; then he grinned like the joke was on him, and he went, too.

"Well," I asked Mark, "what now?"

"We'll put 'em right back," he said, grinning, "and dad won't know but what he just overlooked 'em."

We fixed everything like it was, and then we went down-town to see what we could find out about the stranger.

He was in the hotel when we got there, and it was easy to get out of Bert Sawyer all he knew about him. His name was Henry C. Batten, and he lived in Pittsburg. He was a traveling man for the International Engineering Company, Bert thought, and later we found out it was so, because he left one of his cards in his room and Bert found it.

We sat on the hotel steps until Uncle Ike Bond's bus rattled up to carry folks to the late train. The stranger squeezed through the door and sat down in a corner, looking as if he wasn't pleased with things in general. Uncle Ike winked at Mark.

"How'd you make out?" he whispered.

Mark went up close and told him all about it, and Uncle Ike like to have fallen off the seat laughing.

"What'd I tell you?" he chuckled to nobody in particular. "Ain't he a slick one? Ain't he? Slicker'n greased pole I call him, eh?"

Then he gathered up the lines, but stooped over again to whisper, "If ever this thing gits where you need help from Uncle Ike Bond just up and say so in his hearin', and we'll see what a eddication got on top of a bus is good for."

I didn't see what good he could ever do anybody, but that just shows how you can be mistaken in folks.

CHAPTER V

Right up till snow was on the ground the Ku Klux Klan used to meet in the cave. We would go up there Saturday mornings, all coming by different roads, and when we met there would be passwords and signals and grips and all sorts of secret things. After a while we got so many signs that a fellow had to be pretty careful what he was up to so as not to be telling the other members he was in deadly peril, or that a secret meeting was called at once, or something else, because almost everything we did had a meaning. For instance, if I was to reach around and scratch my back when Mark or Plunk or Binney were looking, that meant that I had to speak to them right away about something important; and if one of us shoved both hands in his pockets at once that meant to look out because enemies were watching. All our signals were simple things like that that wouldn't be noticed. Mark got most of them up, and I guess there were more than a hundred things to be remembered.

We used to sit in the cave and wish there were some real wrongs being done that we could right, or that we had some kind of a powerful enemy, or that there was a mean, miserable whelp that we could visit at night with our white sheets on and tie him to a tree and frighten him into being a good citizen; but there weren't any, and we had to take it out in making believe. But that was almost as much fun.

We had one sign that was never to be used except when we were desperate and needed help and succor, and that was to untie your necktie and tie it up again. But the best one of all was the jack-knife sign, and it was a dandy, because there were so many ways of using it. If one of us met the other and said "Lemme take your jack-knife," that was one way; or if you sent a note by somebody else with the word jack-knife in it, or anything like that. But the best way was the one to be used if you were a captive, or if enemies were surrounding the cave and you wanted to have your comrades rally around you. Nobody would ever suspect it. All you had to do was to meet somebody, a farmer or a man fishing or any one, and give him your knife and tell him please to give it to any one of the society. As soon as that one got the knife he had to collect the others and make for the cave as fast as he could. It worked bully. Lots of times I've sent my little brother over to Mark's with my knife, and dozens of times Mark or Binney or Plunk have sent their knives to me. Once Binney sent his by his father, who was going past my house. I don't believe the real, original Ku-Kluxers had a better sign than that.

The cave was up on the side hill like I told you, and looked down on the river. I told you, too, how Uncle Ike Bond was always fishing when he could get time, which was most always, and he used to come past almost every time we were there. After a while it got so he'd stop to talk to us or we'd go down to talk to him.

Finally one day he grinned, knowing-like, and asked what we were doing there so much.

We looked at one another, and then Mark reached around and scratched his back. That meant, of course, that he had to speak about something important right away, so we got up and told Uncle Ike we'd be back in a minute. He grinned and nodded.

We went off out of earshot, and Mark Tidd whispered:

"Uncle Ike's a pretty good f-f-friend, ain't he?"

We said yes, he was.

"I think he's catchin' on that we're up to somethin'."

"Maybe so," I said.

"Let's make him a m-member. Then he can't give us away. Besides, he'd be a pretty valuable one, anyhow."

We talked it over awhile, and it was decided unanimous to make him a Ku-Kluxer, so we went back to where he was sitting.

"Uncle Ike," says Mark, "can you keep a secret?"

"Wa-all, I hain't never been tempted very hard, but I guess I can keep one good enough for ordinary purposes."

"This is the secretest thing that ever was," says Binney.

"Um!" says Uncle Ike. "You don't tell!"

"We're the Ku Klux Klan," says Plunk, to save Mark the trouble of stuttering so many k's.

"And we want you to join if you'll take the oath."

"Sure," says Uncle Ike. "I've always hankered to b'long to somethin' secret, but I hain't never seemed to git around to it."

Mark recited the oath, and Uncle Ike swore to it solemn as could be. He seemed real glad to be a member. After that we spent most of the afternoon teaching him our secret signs and tokens and things. He said he didn't think he could learn all of them, but that a few dozen of the most important would do. He seemed particular delighted with the jack-knife sign.

"But looky here," he said, shaking his finger in our faces, "don't go workin' any of them signs on me unless you mean 'em in earnest. You young fellers kin fool with 'em as much as you want to, but don't go sendin' me no jack-knives till you git where you need my help and need it bad. I'm too old to go gallivantin' around chasin' wild geese."

After that he stopped to our meetings more often than ever, and pretty nearly every time he'd have a big bass, or maybe a nice mess of pan-fish for us to cook for our dinner. We were all glad we made him a member.

All this while Mr. Tidd was working steady on his turbine, and it was getting nearer and nearer to being ready for a trial to see if the model would work and do what he thought it was going to do. He didn't do anything else but work in the barn and read the *Decline and Fall* and forget things. I mean he didn't have any job, but lived on money that he had in the bank. If it hadn't been for that he'd have had to go on being a machinist all the rest of his life, and probably wouldn't ever have had time to do any inventing.

With all his forgetting and absent-mindedness and inventing he was one of the most patient men. I never heard him speak sharp, and, no matter what happened, good or bad, he took it just the same, not seeming much disturbed; and always simple and kind-spoken to everybody. He always would stop to answer questions or explain things or just talk to us boys if we came into the shop, and never told us to get out or quit bothering him. Nothing bothered him. But Mrs. Tidd wasn't that way. She'd worry and worry, and sometimes when she was flying around up to her ears in work she'd out with something cross, not meaning it at all, but letting it fly off the tip of her tongue. But she was never short with Mr. Tidd and never exasperated with him, no matter what he forgot or did wrong.

All four of us—that is, Mark and Plunk and Binney and me—went out to Mr. Tidd's shop to ask if Mark could come with us and camp Friday night and Saturday and Saturday night and Sunday at our cave. The rest of us had asked and could go if we wanted to. We wanted to, but we didn't want to without Mark.

Mr. Tidd was tinkering and filing and fussing around with some little parts of his turbine, and we had to speak two or three times before he heard us; then he turned around surprised-like and said, "Bless my soul, bless my soul," as if we had just come from a thousand miles away in an airship. He laid down his tools and leaned his arm on his bench and stared at us a minute. Then he said "Bless my soul" again and reached for his handkerchief.

"You've got it tied around your neck," Binney told him.

Mr. Tidd felt and found it where Binney said. "Well, well," he sort of whispered. "However come that there?"

"Pa," began Mark, "can I go camping at the cave? The fellers are goin'."

"Camping," said Mr. Tidd; "camping at the cave? To be sure—at the cave. Um! What cave?"

"Our cave," we all said at once.

We told him all about it, and he was as interested as could be, asking questions and nodding his head and smiling, just like he wanted to go to the cave himself.

"Can I go, pa?" Mark asked, when we were through.

"Far's *I'm* concerned you can," said Mr. Tidd, "but you better ask your ma. She sort of looks after such things. I guess she looks after everything; and, Mark, when you ask her see if she knows where my shoes are. I swan I couldn't find 'em this mornin' when I came out—couldn't find hide nor hair of 'em. It does beat all how things get lost."

Mrs. Tidd was dusting the parlor when we went in, and had a cloth tied around her hair. She was just *flying* around, poking behind things and into corners and going as fast as if she had to have it all done in two minutes.

"Ma," Mark says, poking his head through the door, "can I go campin' with the fellers?"

"No," says Mrs. Tidd, without turning her head. Then she stopped a second and felt of her hair. "What's that you say?"

Mark asked her again, and we chipped in and explained.

"Was ever such a boy!" she said to herself. "Here I got all the cleanin' and dustin', and bread in the oven. Will you be careful and cover up good at night and not get into any mischief?"

Mark nodded.

"What you going to have to eat?"

I told her we'd bake potatoes and have fish and one thing another.

"You sha'n't do no sich thing—gain' without proper food!" And off she flew to the kitchen and got a basket in a jiffy. Into it she put a big chunk of ham, and a loaf of bread and some butter, and a whole pie and half a chocolate cake, and what was left of a pot of baked beans. "There," says she, "I guess that'll keep you from starvin'."

We said good-by and started for the door, but she came running after us. "Mark," she says, "you take these gray blankets, and, mind you, bring them back again or you'll hear from me." Then she kissed him and flew back to her dusting again.

We had all of our things in the front yard, and it didn't take us any time to get them packed on our backs and start for the river. It was only about half an hour's walk, but it took us a little longer to get there on account of Mark, who wanted to rest every little while; but it wasn't really resting he wanted; it was a piece of his mother's cake. We ate it all up before we got to the cave at all.

We got at the cave from the top of the hill and threw our things down on the slope in front. It was a little chilly in the shade, so Mark told us to gather wood for a fire while he packed things away the way they ought to be. I guess we were gone twenty minutes. When we came back everything was just where we left it, and Mark was standing looking into the cave with his face wrinkled up like it gets when he's puzzled.

"Been workin' hard, ain't you?" sings out Plunk.

Usually Mark would have said something back, but this time he didn't. He turned around and asks, "Have any of you been here since last Saturday?"

Nobody had.

"S-somebody's been in the cave."

"How do you know?" I asked him.

"Things been moved around, and some p-p-potaters is gone," he stuttered.

"Let's look," says Binney; and we all crowded in. Mark knew where everything ought to be, even if we didn't, and he told us just what had been touched and what hadn't. "He used the f-fryin'-pan," he grumbled. "Look!"

Sure enough, there was the frying-pan with grease sticking to the bottom, and we never left it that way.

"Wonder who it could have been?" says Plunk.

"Maybe it was Uncle Ike," guessed Binney.

"No," says Mark, "he'd 'a' cleaned the pan."

That was right. We knew he wouldn't leave any dirty dishes around.

Well, it kind of upset us. Of course, the cave wasn't ours, and anybody could come into it that wanted to, but nobody ever did. It was such a little cave that it didn't amount to much to look at, and it was quite a climb; and now here was somebody poking into our things, and it made us pretty sore.

"Probably some feller come along fishin' and happened onto it," Binney guessed.

It didn't do any good to bother about it, so we set to work and packed our things away and got a fire ready to light. In front of the cave was a little patch of sand—white sand crumbled off the sandstone that the cave was carved out of, I guess—and it was there we had our fires and did our cooking. Mark always fixed the fires, because he knew how to pile the sticks and get them to blazing even if the wind was blowing like sixty. Now he was crouched down ready to strike a match when all of a sudden he said something like he was startled.

"What's matter?" I asked him.

He didn't answer, but bent over and looked at something in the sand. Somehow I felt shivery all at once without any reason, and walked over where he was to see what he was looking at. There in the sand was some kind of a footprint; it was a bare foot, but big, bigger than two ordinary men's feet, with the toes growing sort of sideways. I looked at Mark, and he looked at me.

"What made it?" I whispered. For a minute it didn't seem safe to speak out loud.

"I dunno," says Mark, with his eyes big and his face serious. "Looks like a man if the toes weren't on sideways."

We called Plunk and Binney, but they couldn't make anything out of it, so we built the fire good and big, just in case it was some kind of a wild animal. We knew animals were afraid of fire.

It was Binney who thought about the frying-pan. "It must be a man, or it wouldn't have used the pan," he says.

That was right. Animals don't cook. Plunk drew a long breath. "Maybe it's a wild man," he said, trembly voiced.

"Like there was with that circus last summer," I said, remembering the pictures in front of the tent of seven men catching a thing all hair and beard, with skins on it for clothes, and big teeth. We all got closer to the fire.

"Bosh!" snorts Mark; but his voice was a little dry, and he didn't look any too comfortable. "There ain't any wild men." But he didn't believe it and we didn't believe it.

"What had we better do?" asks Binney.

"Nothing," says Plunk, letting on he wasn't afraid. "It won't hurt anybody even if it is a wild man. And, besides, there are four of us."

That wasn't so very encouraging, judging from the size of the footprint. Anything with a foot as big as that could take four boys at a bite.

"Had we better stay?" Binney was pretty scared and showed it.

"Of course," Plunk told him. "We ain't babies. We got to stay."

We couldn't very well back down after that. I expect every one of us was willing enough to pack up and go, but nobody would start it, so we sat close to the blaze and talked about other things, and made believe to one another that wild men were the last thing in the world we'd ever think of running away from.

It began to get dark, and we cooked supper. It wasn't a very cheerful meal because every once in a while one of us would stop to listen and ask, "What was that?" There were lots of noises, like there always are in the woods, but they never seemed so shivery before. The moon didn't come up till late, and it was dark as a pocket except where our fire lighted things up for a few feet.

"We ought to have a gun," said Plunk, after we had been quiet a long time.

"Bosh!" said Mark. "Let's go to b-b-bed."

"We got to have a guard," says Binney. "The Ku Klux Klan wouldn't camp without a sentinel."

We agreed to that. The night was divided into watches, and we drew pieces of stick to show who would watch first. I drew the shortest piece, and the other fellows went into the cave and wrapped themselves up in their blankets. I sat out by the fire, and I can tell you it was pretty lonesome and scary.

CHAPTER VI

After a while I could hear Mark snoring inside the cave, and it made me sort of mad. Anybody would think he'd been brought up next-door neighbor to a wild man or whatever kind of a thing it was that went around leaving marks in the sand a foot long, with the toes turned toward the side. I crept over to the opening and looked in. All three of them were asleep, and if I felt lonely and skittish before I pretty nearly went into a panic now. The fire was going good, but I threw on more wood just to have something to do and to light up farther into the woods.

Pretty soon the moon came up, and that made it seem chillier. It was as if the light was cold—it looked as if it was. I edged closer to the fire, where the blaze almost scorched my shins, and crouched there, with my heart beating thump, thump, and my insides feeling as if they were shriveling together for lack of anything to hold them out like they ought to be. I looked at my watch, hoping my turn on guard was over. Only a little more than a half-hour of it was gone!

The moon got higher, and the woods, instead of just being black as if a curtain was hanging all around me, got shadowy, and the shadows moved. Give me black darkness any time to the kind where there are patches of light and patches of shadows that keep shifting and oozing around; when the woods look that way you feel certain something is hiding and watching you in the places where the light isn't.

I got the hatchet and put it between my knees, but it didn't make me feel much better. I tried whittling, but I couldn't keep my eyes on it; they wanted to wander around to see if anything was sneaking up on me. I thought about lots of things, and one of them was that if ever I got home it would take a lot of persuading to get me camping out at night again.

Another half an hour went by, and it seemed as if my hours would never pass. Nothing happened, but sometimes I wished it would. Being afraid something will happen is worse than the thing itself if it comes.

I guess it was about half-past ten when the funniest feeling came over me. It's hard to tell just what it was, but more than anything else it felt as if somebody's eyes were bearing on my back, watching and watching; and it felt as if the eyes were bright and as if they'd shine in the dark if I was to turn and look at them. I sat for more than five minutes before I could get up courage to look. When I did I couldn't see a thing, but, all the same, I was as sure as anything that something had been looking at me.

About fifteen minutes later I heard a noise; it was just as if somebody had slipped on the hillside and scrambled for a minute before he could catch his feet. It might have been a stray sheep, or maybe a coon roaming around in the moonlight, but it didn't sound like it to me; it sounded bigger and stronger. It was so very still afterward that I was more afraid than ever, because if it *had* been a sheep I'd have heard him running away, and even a coon would have made some sort of a racket. No, I says to myself, it's something hiding and sneaking around with an eye on us; it's the thing that used our pan and stole our potatoes and left that track in the sand.

That was all that happened during my watch, but I was glad when it came time to wake Mark to take my place. He came out rubbing his eyes and blinking at the light.

"Talk to me a minute," he yawned, "till I git awake."

We talked a spell, but I didn't say anything about the noise or that I thought something had been watching me. When he was awake so he wouldn't doze off again I went in and snuggled into my blanket. I was afraid at first I wouldn't be able to get to sleep, but before I really got to worrying about it I was gone; and I didn't dream, either.

In the morning none of us had much to say about his watch during the night. By the looks of the others I'm sure they were just as afraid as I was, but they weren't letting on and neither was I. Besides, it seemed sort of foolish with the sunlight shining bright through the trees and the water glittering and the birds chittering all around. The woods didn't look as if there could be anything fearsome or dangerous in them; wild men seemed a long ways away and nothing to worry about, anyhow. What would a wild man be doing right outside of Wicksville? If there was one somebody would have seen it and talked about it before we got there.

We fished all day and played Indian and fixed up a raft out of a couple of old logs and poled ourselves around. In the afternoon we went over on the island and gathered about a bushel of butternuts apiece, but they weren't any good, having laid all winter.

"We'll have h-h-ham for supper," Mark said. "We kin warm it up, and it'll be pretty good with fish."

We poled the raft across, carrying our nuts, and made for the cave. Mark went to work building the fire again, Plunk and Binney gathered wood, while I riffled around inside getting things ready for the cooking. I found most of the stuff all right, because Mark had put it away, and he always puts things away careful, but when it came to the ham I couldn't put my hand on it to save my life.

"Where did you put that ham?" I sang out to Mark.

"Right in that jar," he told me, "next to the basket."

"It ain't here," I called, after I had looked again to make sure.

"It's got to be," says he, his voice a little excited, "because I put it there."

"Well, it ain't. Come and see for yourself."

He came in and rummaged around, but not a sign of the ham could he discover. His face was sober when he looked up at me and says, "Is anythin' else m-missin'?"

Together we went over the things. Everything was there till we got to the bread. All together we had four loaves. We'd used most of one, and there ought to have been three left, but there wasn't. There were only two.

"Did you hear anything last night?" asks Mark, sharp-like.

"Yes," I says. "Did you?"

"I ain't sure, but I th-thought so."

"I felt somethin' watchin' me," I told him. "Seemed like its eyes was just borin' into me when my back was turned."

"Um!" he grunts. "See anythin'?"

"No."

"Me neither."

"There's somebody prowlin' around, that's sure. That ham didn't git tired of stayin' an' run off alone."

Mark grinned. Then he looked solemn again and nodded.

"Don't seem very dangerous, though—stealin' ham. Maybe somebody's playin' a joke on us."

"Nobody'd hang around all night and all day for this much joke."

He admitted that was right. "But 'tain't no wild man," he insisted. "There ain't none."

"I dunno," I says.

And then Binney and Plunk came along with their arms stacked full of wood.

Mark and I kept quiet before them, but we arranged that we'd keep watch tonight by twos instead of all alone. "It'll be more sociable," I says; and they jumped at the idea.

Mark and I were to stand guard the first part of the night, and Binney and Plunk would be on watch till morning. That was the way it was fixed. About nine o'clock they turned in, and we went out by the fire.

"Let's be sure there's enough wood," I said to him. "I'd sort of hate to be left out here in the dark."

He grunted, but I noticed he looked at the pile pretty careful, and even dragged in some pieces that were lying within reach.

For maybe an hour we got along fine. Not a thing happened, and we found lots of things to talk about. We got to figuring about his father's turbine and what it would do and how much money Mr. Tidd would make out of it, and it sounded pretty important. Some day we were sure there'd be big shops in Wicksville where the engines would be manufactured, and Mark would be general manager when he got through college, and all the rest of us would have good jobs. I was going to be a mechanical engineer some day, so Mark agreed to put me in charge of that department. We figured his father would make maybe four or five thousand dollars in a single year.

"If he m-makes anything," said Mark.

"But he's goin' to."

"He ain't got it patented yet."

"What of it?"

"If somebody got holt of his idee, or stole his drawin's and got it patented f-f-first, he'd never git a thing out of it."

"Not a dollar?"

"Not a dollar. There's always folks tryin' to steal inventions. Most inventors git cheated out of their money or s-some-thin'."

THERE, CROUCHING ON THE BROW, WAS THE FIGURE OF A MAN

"Your father better be pretty careful, then," I says.

"Careful!" grunts Mark. "You know how careful he is—and that feller was in town again."

"No," I says, surprised, for I'd never heard of it before.

"He was, but f-father was out of town. He didn't git no satisfaction."

"I bet he's sneakin' around Wicksville just a-tryin' to gouge that invention out of your father," I says.

Mark didn't answer, and sat so quiet I turned to look at him to see what was the matter. He was sitting stiff, leaning forward a little and staring at the face of a big rock half-way down the hill. There was a shadow on it, and it was the shadow of a man's head.

The moon was shining bright and throwing shadows just like it did the night before. I noticed now that a big shadow was right over us, reaching down the hill to the rock, where it ended in the head. It looked big as an elephant. Mark sucked in his breath, and we looked at each other. Then we both turned slow and looked up the hill. There, crouching on the brow, was the black figure of a man, like he was on his hands and knees staring over at us. His head stood out sharp, and we could see his hair was long and bushy, standing out on all sides just like some kind of South Sea Island savages that there are pictures of in the geography. There wasn't any doubt about his being big. It was the whoppingest head I ever saw, and the shoulders matched it for size.

All of a sudden as we looked the man wasn't there. It seemed like he melted right away under our eyes, and we never heard a sound.

"It was—nothing but a man," I whispered, trying to persuade myself there wasn't any danger.

"Yes," Mark whispered back, "but what k-kind of a man?"

When we got to thinking about his size and how long and bushy his hair was, and especially about that queer footmark with the toes pointing to one side, we couldn't make head or tail of him, except that there was something mighty strange, and that it would be a good thing to keep out of his way. I tell you it wasn't fun sitting there a couple of miles from a house, without a gun, and with a giant of a man like that prowling around watching you and intending to do nobody knew what.

"Shall we tell the others?" I asked.

Mark thought a minute. "No," he says. "'Twon't do no good. We'll keep mum."

That is what we did. When our watch was over we waked Plunk and Binney, and they came out to the fire yawning and stretching. We turned in.

I don't know when it was, but I was woke up by a yelling and hollering outside the cave. Mark and I jumped out, and there were Plunk and Binney screeching as if they were scared to death and throwing blazing chunks of wood out among the trees after a big black figure that ran and leaped and crashed down the hill and out of sight.

"What was it?" I said, shaking Binney by the shoulder.

"I—I guess," he said, shaking like a leaf, "that it was a goriller. He didn't look like anythin' else."

A gorilla! Come to think of it, it *might* be a gorilla, but where in time would one of them come from?

Anyhow, there was no more sleep that night. We all sat up together and kept the fire roaring and blazing as bright as we could. We weren't troubled again.

In the morning Binney says, while we were getting breakfast, "I guess we better go home."

Plunk didn't say anything, and I waited for Mark.

"I ain't goin' home," he says. "I'm goin' to f-find out what it is. Will you stay with me, Tallow?"

"Sure," I says, but I didn't want to a bit.

That sort of shamed Plunk and Binney into staying, so nobody went home.

"And, rem-member," Mark warned us, "this is a secret. We ain't to say a word to nobody."

So we were sort of forced to stay by Mark to help him find out what was prowling around in the woods. He was a queer fellow, Mark was. I know he was as afraid as any of us, but he was curious, and when he got curious to know anything you couldn't scare him away nohow.

CHAPTER VII

"Have you hatched a scheme?" I asked Mark, after we'd scoured off the dishes and cleaned up in front of the cave.

"I got a scheme, but I don't like it much."

"Won't it work?"

"I guess it'll work."

"What's wrong with it, then? You want one that'll work, don't you?"

"I ain't sure," says he, with a grin. "Sometimes it ain't desirable to c-catch what you're after. I dunno just what I'd do with a wild man if I was to get him."

"You might sell him to a circus," says Binney, who always took things serious, and couldn't see a joke if the point was printed out for him.

"What's the scheme?" I was getting pretty impatient to know.

"Make believe we've gone away," says Mark. "Then he'll come prowlin' around. Three of us go over to the island and holler and raise a r-racket. One will stay in the cave. He'll think we're all gone."

"It's a good scheme," I says, "for the feller that stays in the cave."

"That's the trouble," Mark grins.

"Who d'you think'll be fool enough to stay in the cave to catch Mister Wild Man?"

"Me," says Mark.

"You dassen't."

"That's what I'm wonderin'," he owns up.

We sat a while without saying a word, then Mark clicks his teeth and says, "I'm goin' to try it."

"You ain't," I says. "He'll bust you in two."

"I don't b'lieve so. At any rate, I don't in daylight."

"You ain't foolin'?"

"N-no."

"And you want us to go over to the island and kick up a row like there was four of us, so's he'll think nobody's here?"

"Yes."

"Come on, fellers," I says. "If Mark's gump enough to play he's bait in a bear-trap I guess we can kick up his racket for him." We got up and started down hill, leaving Mark in front of the cave looking after us sort of regretful. We weren't more than half-way down before I began to feel on bad terms with myself. Somehow it didn't look just right to go off deserting Mark, especially after binding ourselves to stick together in whatever peril come when we made up the Ku Klux Klan.

"Wait a minute," I told Binney and Plunk. "This ain't no way to do. You fellers got to yell loud enough for four; can you do it?"

"I guess so," says Plunk. "Why?"

"'Cause I'm goin' back to stick with Mark," I grunted, kind of sharp. "There ain't nobody in Wicksville goin' to say I ain't got as much sand as Mark Tidd."

"I sha'n't go back," Binney says. "I didn't ask him to stay."

"Me too," agreed Plunk.

"Nobody asked you to go back. Somebody's got to do the hollerin' on the island, ain't they? Well, all you got to do is sound like a whole picnic. Now git."

I went back up the hill cautious and sneaking and sat down just back of Mark. He didn't hear me till I slipped, and then the way he jumped reminded me of a big rubber ball bounding.

"Whillisker!" he panted, "but you scairt me!"

"Too bad. If I scairt you what'll the wild man do?"

He grinned kind of sickly. "What you doin' here?"

"I come to stay," I says. "Plunk and Binney can make enough row."

He looked pretty thankful, but tried not to show it. "There ain't no need," he says.

"If you don't want me I'll git out," I told him.

He grinned again. "I dunno's I'd go as far's kickin' you out. If you're g-goin' to stay let's git inside the cave."

We went inside and fixed ourselves as comfortable as we could at the far end, in a sort of recess we'd dug out to put things in, with a piece of canvas hanging down over it, and all the talking we did was in whispers. Somehow we didn't either of us think of many things to say. I remember after about half an hour of it that I wished if any wild man was coming he'd hurry and have it over with, because my legs were getting cramped. But he didn't come.

Through the mouth of the cave we could hear Plunk and Binney raising a racket that sounded as if all the kids in Wicksville were mixed up in one big fight.

"They're doin' fine," whispers Mark.

"Yes," I says, "and I bet they're enjoyin' it more'n I am this."

It began to look as if Mark's scheme wasn't any good, for we sat there more than two hours, and I was sure my legs would snap off if I moved, they were so stiff.

"Come on," I whispered, "let's get out of this. Nobody's comin'."

"*Hus-ss-ssh!*"

I listened. Sure enough, there was something moving around outside, slow and cautious. We could hear twigs crackling, and once in a while a sort of scuffling like feet moving through dried grass. Mark's eyes were fastened on the opening through a slit in the canvas, and they were pretty nearly as big as saucers. When you think how small his eyes usually were you can guess how excited he was now. Probably I looked about the same; I know my heart hammered, and I got that empty feeling like I had in the night, and I wished I was seven miles away with a company of soldiers. But I wasn't any place but right there, and I had to make the best of it.

The sounds came nearer and nearer and nearer until whoever made them was right outside. Then the opening was darkened, and we could see a big head and shoulders that were as broad as the hole. The head stopped and peered around to make sure nobody was there. We were way in the corner; it was pretty dark, and the canvas was in front of us. So there wasn't much chance of his seeing us or finding us. He mumbled something to himself and crept way in. I almost hollered right out. He was the biggest man I ever saw, and wild-looking. We couldn't see his face very well, but he was ragged, and his hair was long and frowsy—and we were alone with him in a little cave, and nobody to help within a couple of miles.

He crawled in on all fours and began fumbling around on the other side of the cave where we had kept the bread. I felt Mark heave himself up, and then saw him creep out of the blankets and across the floor until he was between the door and the wild man. It took more nerve than I had, but, though he was as pale as a sheet, he kept right ahead. He stood still, kind of doubtful, getting up his courage to do something and figuring out just what he was going to do. I felt around for something heavy I could use if worse came to worst.

Mark opened his mouth once, but not a sound came. He shut it again and felt of his throat; then he made his voice sound as deep and heavy as he could and sort of barked: "Hey! W-what you do-doin' here?"

The wild man jumped so he cracked his head against the roof and turned around rubbing it. For the first time we got a good look at his face when the light from outside struck it fair. I expected he was going to leap right at Mark till I saw his face; and then, somehow, I felt sorry for him and not afraid a bit, for it was the most scared face I ever saw—yes, sir, scared! He fairly cowered against the wall.

"Don't hurt Sammy. Poor Sammy. Sammy's hungry," he whimpered.

Mark and I both giggled, we were so relieved. Mark spoke to him again like he was stern and displeased.

"What you stealin' our stuff for? Hey?"

"Sammy's hungry," said the wild man again. "Don't hurt Sammy."

He turned his great, round, simple face to Mark, his big eyes, blue as a baby's, full of trouble. He smiled like a child will that has been bad and thinks it can get out of it by being specially friendly.

"Come outside," orders Mark, "where there's more room."

We went out on the sand, Mark first, the wild man second, and me last. Out there he could stand up straight, and I tell you when he did I was glad he was so simple and good-natured, and not wild and savage like the pictures in front of the side-show. I'm pretty well grown for my age, but I couldn't have reached to the top of his head even standing tiptoe. My father is six foot one, so I'm used to seeing a big man, but our wild man must have been a head taller than dad. Afterward we got him to let us measure him, and he turned out to be six foot six and a half—almost tall enough to be a giant in a museum. And he was broad, too. When he turned his back it looked as wide as a dining-room table.

His face was round and innocent, like I said before, and good-natured. His hair was black as Mr. Whittaker's stallion and as coarse as the horse's tail—coarse and straight. Take it and his smooth, coppery skin, and we made sure he was an Indian. He was, almost.

He was all ragged, with great holes torn in his clothes. I looked at his feet. One of them had a shoe on, and the other was bare. The bare one was the foot that had scared us so when we saw its print in the sand by the cave with the toes pointing sideways. Now we understood, for that foot was twisted and sort of crumpled up like it had been hurt a long time ago and healed wrong. But with all that he hardly limped a bit, and how he could run!

"Don't send Sammy back," he begged. "Sammy wants to stay here. Don't tell on Sammy."

"Back where?" asks Mark.

"Back to the big farm. Sammy ran away.... They make Sammy sleep in the house, and they make him dig and work, and they won't ever let him go fishing. Don't send Sammy back."

"He means the poor-farm, I guess," I said to Mark; and he nodded.

"How did you get sent to the poor-farm?"

Sammy always spoke about himself as if he were somebody else. I never heard him say "I" as long as I have known him. It made him seem very simple and childish and feeble-minded, but Sammy knew and thought a whole lot more than folks gave him credit for. He knew how many apples it took to make six, all right, and lots of things besides. But, after all, he was just like a little boy, a little frightened boy with a great big body.

He told us all about himself, and it was so interesting to listen to that we clean forgot all about Plunk and Binney and dinner until he was through. He said he was born in a lumber camp that used to be in the neighborhood a good many years ago, before the pine was cut off. His father was half French and half Indian, and his mother was mostly Indian. He couldn't remember much about being little, because he wasn't very old when he got hurt some way with a falling tree or a log on a rollway or something, and it almost killed him. That's how he got his twisted foot, and probably he got a knock on the head that spoiled his brains.

For a long time he lived with his father in a little shack over beyond Loon Lake, which was about seven miles away, and nobody had bothered him. He and his father had fished and hunted and one thing and another so as to get enough to eat. Then his father died and left Sammy all alone. He got along pretty good until winter, and it was a hard winter, so that there wasn't much hunting, and he almost starved. When he came into town to get something to eat, begging, they clapped him into jail and then sent him off to the poor-farm.

It took him a long time to tell all of this, because every little while he'd stop and look at us pitiful and beg us not to tell on him or send him back, and then he'd go on again, but all the time he kept his eyes on us and started nervous-like whenever a twig snapped or a bird peeped back in the woods.

"Well," says Mark, "I s'pose you're a sort of wild man; but I'm glad you ain't the kind we thought you were."

"Sammy's nice. Everybody like Sammy, sure."

"About sendin' him back," I says to Mark, "it ain't goin' to be done. He's Injun, and the woods and things is for Injuns, not poorfarms. He hadn't ought to be shut up no more than a robin or a chipmunk, and he ain't goin' to be if I can help it."

Sammy looked at me out of his big eyes so grateful I had to blink, and then he reached out with his great paw and patted the back of my hand.

"Boy good to Sammy," he said. "Kind in his heart to poor Sammy."

"Sure," I told him; and there was a kind of a chunk in my throat.

"No," says Mark, "he ain't goin' back. We'll hide him and p-p-purtect him and shield him from his enemies."

"Enemies?" I says. "He ain't got no enemies that I know of. The folks at the poor-farm ain't his enemies; they're tryin' to be kind to him."

"Rats!" he snaps, disgusted as could be. "Maybe they ain't enemies one way of lookin' at it, but we kin play they are."

"I s'pose so."

"Anyhow, we won't tell, and we'll help him all we can."

Sammy smiled so he showed all his white, even teeth, and bobbed his head at Mark.

"Fat boy good. Sammy like fat boy—sure."

"I s'pose they'll be lookin' for him," I guessed.

"'Tain't likely they'll strain theirselves," Mark says. "All Sammy's got to do is lay l-low."

"He can live in our cave."

"Sammy live in cave—sure. Roll in blanket and sleep. Catch fish in river, shoot, hunt."

"You haven't any gun."

He looked real crafty and half closed his eyes while he bobbed his head back and forth. "Sammy got gun—sure. Good gun."

All of a sudden we remembered Plunk and Binney, and I jumped up and put my hands to my mouth to holler at them, but I happened to glance at Sammy, who looked like he was ready to jump and run, so I stopped and explained to him. He quieted down, and then I hollered. I had to holler two or three times before I got an answer, but after a while I could hear them hooting back at me. I told them to come on, and in about five minutes they came tearing up the hill. I guess they never expected to see us again, the way they looked. And surprised!—you never saw anything like it. They were a little sorry, too, that they hadn't stayed. You see, nobody'd got hurt, and they might as well have had the credit for being brave. That's the way with lots of folks. They can figure out after the time is passed what they ought to have done the week before.

Well, we held a meeting of the Ku Klux Klan right there, and voted Sammy our ward. Mark found out he was that. Indians, he said, were the wards of the nation, and ward meant somebody that was looked after and taken care of, so he guessed that's what Sammy was to us. Sammy was agreeable, and grinned and grinned and bobbed his head and said "Sure, sure, sure" every little while.

It was getting about time for us to go home, so we left Sammy all the things to eat and as many dishes as we dared, and told him we'd be back to see him in a day or two and bring more grub. Then we shook hands all round, and off we went with the first real big secret we'd ever had, and I tell you we felt pretty important over it.

CHAPTER VIII

If we'd known what a trouble Sammy was going to be to us all through the winter, I guess we'd have been more careful about making him our ward. But we'd done it, and there was nothing for us but to stand by him—and he did have a monstrous appetite. After winter came on we pretty nearly had to feed him. He did get things to eat besides what we took him—chicken sometimes, I guess, and things like that. We never asked how he got them, and he never told us, but I don't imagine it was best for folks in that neighborhood to leave things laying after dark.

We were afraid he'd freeze to death, but the cold never seemed to bother him. In the cave he had some old quilts and a piece of carpet he used to hang across the opening to shut out the wind. When he built a fire on the sand before the cave it was surprising how warm it got inside, and then he'd drop his curtain, and it seemed like the heat would stay for hours after the fire was gone.

Of course, he couldn't stay in the cave all the time, and, though we cautioned him, he did go prowling around the country a good deal, even on the roads. Once or twice he was seen at night, and one farmer came lashing his horse into town with a story of being chased by a ghost twenty feet high with hair two yards long. We knew who the ghost was, all right, though we couldn't see why Sammy chased the man. He told us it was just for fun. That's the way he was, a regular little boy, and how he did love to play pranks! What with him sneaking around that section and with people missing things and catching glimpses of him in the darkness, the locality got a bad name. It doesn't take long for a place to get a bad name; and, no matter how much folks don't believe in ghosts, they're ready to believe in something or other. I don't believe in them, and Mark says there isn't any such thing, but all the same there are times when the chills run all over you and you know there's something that isn't flesh and blood right behind you.

All that winter we lugged things to eat out to the cave, usually a couple of times a week, and when the drifts were high it was pretty hard work. But Sammy was always grateful, and when you come to think about what came later, and how valuable Sammy was to us, I shouldn't wonder if he was worth more than our trouble.

During the winter Mr. Tidd worked harder than ever on his turbine, and before the last snow was off the ground he had his working model, or whatever he called it, about ready for a trial. He was excited and we were excited, but it was Mark that thought of something that gave us all a setback.

"How you goin' to try it? You ain't got any s-steam."

Mr. Tidd scratched his head and looked at Mark reproachful-like, as if calling his attention to it was as bad as if Mark had come right up and taken steam away from him that he'd been saving for the purpose.

"It won't run without steam," he said, slow and worried. "Without steam a-sissin' and strainin' and workin' it won't do nothin'. It might just as well be a bag of potaters for all the good it is. Well, well! Um!" After a minute he brightened up like he always did. Worry and Mr. Tidd never could stay together long. "There's some way out of it," he said, "some way out of it. The trouble—the trouble seems to be, now I think of it, that no way comes into my head."

He sighed and pulled a volume of the *Decline and Fall* out of his pocket and commenced to read. In less than a minute he'd forgotten all about us and the turbine and the steam and everything else in the world but those old Roman folks that went tearing and rampaging all over the world without much regard for anybody's feelings, so I've always thought. How Mr. Tidd, a gentle, nice man, could be fond of such characters as those Romans was a mystery to me. He used to read pieces out of the *Decline and Fall* to us, and in the course of a year I calculate we heard most all of it. I can't remember that those folks ever did anything but fight. From morning till night they were picking on somebody. What I'd like to know is, if the whole nation was always fighting, who tended the post-office and ran the stores and looked after things at home? Quite likely the womenfolks had to do that while their husbands were gallivanting around in Gaul or Egypt or other foreign parts. To my mind those Romans were a ridiculous lot.

"If you haven't got steam here," I said, trying to puzzle it out, "I guess you'll have to take your model where steam is."

"What's that?" Mr. Tidd asked, looking up from his book. "What's that? Oh yes. Of course."

"Don't you know anybody that's got steam that'll lend some to you?"

Mr. Tidd thought. Then he slapped his knee. "There's Mr. Whiteley over at the power-plant. Him and me has got pretty friendly, one way and another. He's got steam. Now, do you s'pose he'd be willin'? Do you?"

"I don't see why he shouldn't," I told him; and Mark nodded his head once or twice to show he agreed.

The upshot of it was that Mr. Tidd went to see Mr. Whiteley and got permission to set up his turbine in a corner of the room where the engines and things were to give it a trial. When we found that out—I mean Binney and Plunk and me—we were all as wrought up about it as though it was our father doing the inventing.

Mr. Tidd put in about a week finishing his turbine and setting it up in the engine-room. We went down to see it when it was all ready. It was to be tried out the next morning. Tucked away in a corner of the engine-room it didn't look like much. It was little and boxed in so you couldn't see any of the machine parts that made it go, and somehow didn't seem very important when you compared it with the big wheels and beams and one thing and another on the engine that stood, all shining with brass, in the middle of the floor. We felt a sort of sinking.

But Mr. Tidd was humming and happy. He patted his little contraption and beamed and beamed. Then he'd look over at the big engine and smile scornful-like. "This here leetle feller," he said, "will do most as much work as you will, with all your size and brass and roarin'. You want to look out, for this leetle feller is goin' to be the death of you, and don't you forget it!"

"Mr. Tidd," said Mr. Whiteley, "I hope you aren't too confident. It won't be too big a disappointment if it fails to work?"

"Fails to work! Why, it *will* work, Mr. Whiteley. It—"

"But lots of others have failed—men with technical educations, eminent engineers."

"They didn't know what I know, Mr. Whiteley. Not what I know. No, sir. The Tidd turbine's goin' to do what it ought to. You see."

We left the engine-room, and Mark went home with his father. The trial was to come off at nine o'clock the next morning, and we were to be there. It was a promise. Nobody was to see it but Mr. Tidd and Mr. Whiteley and us four boys. Of course the engineer would be there, but he didn't count—or we thought so, anyhow.

Binney and I were on hand before eight o'clock, and we had a whole hour to hang around. It was tiresome waiting by the door, so we got up and prowled around the building just to pass away the time and see what we could see. After a while we got tired and sat down on a plank that ran across a couple of oil barrels under a window of the engine-room and made ourselves comfortable. The window was open, and I could hear voices inside, but I supposed it was the engineer talking to some of his help and didn't think anything about it until whoever it was came closer. It was the engineer, all right, but I couldn't make out from the sound who was with him, though there was something familiar about the voice.

"They're goin' to turn steam into the thing at nine o'clock," said the engineer. "Funny-lookin' contraption, ain't it?"

"Um!" said the other man. "Why didn't you telegraph me sooner?"

"I didn't know when they was goin' to be ready until yestiddy. Soon's I found out I sent off a wire right off. Anyhow, you're here, ain't you?"

"Yes," said the man, in a kind of a grunt. "What d'you s'pose is inside the thing?"

"Hain't got no idee. What are you so all-fired int'rested in it for? You don't reckon this coot of a Tidd has up and invented somethin', do you?"

"You can never tell, my friend," said the man; and all at once I recognized his voice. It was the same man that we saw on the depot platform and that tried to get Mr. Tidd to show him his drawings and patterns and things last fall—the fellow that worked for some machinery company in Pittsburg.

"Confound it," he went on, snappishly, "he's got it all covered up with casing so's you can't see into it at all. Wonder what his idea *is*. Can't we pry into it and see?"

I calculated it was about time to do something, so I stuck my head in the window and hollered, like I'd just got there, "Hey, Mr. Willis"—which was the engineer's name—"open the door, will you please? Mr. Tidd'll be here in a minute, and we want to git in."

I saw the stranger kick the floor like he was mighty mad, but there wasn't anything Mr. Willis could do but let us in, so he didn't get to see into the engine that time. When we got inside the stranger was gone.

"Somebody with you, wasn't there?" I asked Mr. Willis.

He grunted out a yes, and then jerked his head back through the engine-room. "Feller tryin' to sell oil. He just went out the other way."

"Oh," I says; but I didn't believe he was selling oil or that he was gone very far away. You don't telegraph men to come and try to sell you things.

It wasn't more than five minutes before Mr. Tidd and Mark and Plunk came in with Mr. Whiteley.

"Everything ready?" Mr. Whiteley asked the engineer; and Willis nodded that it was. Mr. Tidd went over to his turbine and began fiddling around with it, and I grabbed Mark by the arm and whispered in his ear, "That feller's here."

"What feller?"

"The sneakin' one. That one that's after your father's turbine. He's hidin' here somewheres. The engineer's a friend of his'n and telegraphed him to come."

"Sure?" Mark asked, sharp.

"I saw him and heard him."

Mark took hold of his fat cheek with his finger and thumb and pinched it. His little eyes were going here and there around the machinery and into corners, and he was thinking hard.

"He's hidin' where he can s-s-see," he says, half to himself.

"Of course," I told him, "that's what he came for."

Now, if it had been me I'd have told Mr. Tidd and Mr. Whiteley right off and had the stranger put out; but that wasn't Mark's way. He always wanted to engineer things differently and be original about it. If there was an easy way, like there was now, and some other way that had to be puzzled and figured over, he'd choose that way every time. I knew there wasn't any use in my saying anything, so I just waited to see what would happen.

"I dunno's it will do any harm if he d-does see it run. He can't find out nothin'. Maybe it's a good thing he came. Havin' him sneakin' round like this may show father he ain't to be trusted. Eh?"

I could see there was something in that. If we could get it into Mr. Tidd's head that all the world wasn't as honest as a prayer-meeting we'd be doing something pretty valuable.

"It's your business," I told him, "and you can run it the way you want to."

He kept peering around cautious, and finally he decided the stranger was hiding in one of two places. One of them was a sort of toolroom right across from where we stood; the other place was a dark cubbyhole under the stairs. He could see all right from either place.

Mr. Tidd was all ready now to begin his trial. He told the engineer to turn on his steam, and we all stood around, almost forgetting to breathe. We could see the steam climbing up in the gauge he'd fixed until it showed there was a hundred pounds of pressure.

"There," he says, "that's enough. Now we're agoin' to see the Tidd turbine set about its business. There's no doubt about it; not a mite."

"Don't be too confident," warns Mr. Whiteley.

Mr. Tidd only smiled and turned a little thing that let the steam into his turbine. Pretty soon there came a sort of purring like a cat, only not so loud; maybe it was more like the whirring of an electric fan. We couldn't see the machine shake or anything, and it didn't look to me like a thing had happened. But Mr. Tidd was dancing up and down, and saying "I told you so!" and slapping his hip with his big hand, and acting in general like he had gone crazy.

Mr. Whiteley looked at him sort of queer, like he was afraid he really had gone out of his head, and says: "Hold hard; Tidd, get a grip on yourself. She may work yet."

Mr. Tidd stopped capering and stared at Mr. Whiteley with his mouth open. "May work yet!" he says. "May work yet! Ho, ho! May work yet! Do you hear that hummin', Mr. Whiteley, and that purrin'? And, Mr. Whiteley, do you see that shaft a-turnin'? Ho, ho! I knew it!"

"Do you mean the thing's working?" demanded Mr. Whiteley.

"She's a-turnin' her rotator this very second about twelve thousand times a minute," says Mr. Tidd, "and she's a-stirrin' up close to a hundred horse-power."

"Impossible!" says Mr. Whiteley.

"Measure it, then," sings Mr. Tidd. "Measure it."

The engineer brought Mr. Whiteley a couple of little brass things, and he hitched them onto the turbine. The one that measured the revolutions seemed to go plum crazy for a while, then it settled down to business, and Mr. Whiteley bent over to read what it said. He rubbed his eyes and looked again. "Tidd," he said, all excited, "Tidd, it can't be possible! It can't! But this says you're making fourteen thousand revolutions to the minute."

"What's she doin' in the way of horse-power?" Mr. Tidd chuckled.

Mr. Whiteley fussed around a while till he found out.

"It says the machine's turning up one hundred and two horse-power," he says, kind of hushed like. With that he walked over to Mr. Tidd and put out his hand. "Mr. Tidd," says he, "you've done it. You've come close to revolutionizing the business of applying power, and you're going to be a rich man."

"Wait," says Mr. Tidd. "You hain't seen it all. What's one of the greatest obstacles now in the turbine?"

"The difficulty of reversing."

"Watch," says Mr. Tidd. He turned a cock one place and turned another at the opposite end. "There," says he; "she's reversed."

"What!" Mr. Whiteley said, his face all twisted up with astonishment.

"Fact," grins Mr. Tidd. "Fact, gen-*u*-ine fact. As sure as that Cæsar conquered Gaul." "Have you got your patent?"

"Nope. Couldn't get it till I proved she'd work. But I'm goin' to git it quick now, you can bet, perty sudden."

Mark sort of scrooged up to his father. "Father," he says, "come here a minute. I want to show you and Mr. Whiteley somethin'."

They looked at him surprised-like.

"Over here." Mark points.

He walks to the toolroom and points. "Here it is," he says, "a-crouchin' in here. C-come out!" he tells the stranger.

The stranger, seeing there wasn't anything else to do, did come out looking flustered and a little greasy where he'd squeezed up against things. "What's this?" snaps Mr. Whiteley. "What are you doing here?"

The man didn't say anything for a minute, and I noticed the engineer was looking pretty uncomfortable. Mark spoke right up, though.

"He was sneakin' around to see father's engine work. He's been s-s-spyin' around a year, he has. He works for some engineerin' company in Pittsburg."

"I *have* been watching Mr. Tidd's progress with his turbine," said the stranger, in a make-believe honest kind of voice. "I represent capital, and Mr. Tidd will need capital to market and manufacture his invention. It was my desire to see how he came out before I raise his hopes by offering him financial support."

"It was a queer way you took," Mr. Whiteley said, and his voice sounded unpleasant. "You've found out it works, all right. *Now git!*" He took a step forward, and the stranger looked like he was startled plenty. He didn't wait to make any more explanations, but hurried out of the engine-room.

"Tidd," said Mr. Whiteley, "you want to look out. The best thing you can do is to get off after your patent and protect yourself. If you don't you'll just be another inventor cheated out of the profits of his invention—and yours is a big one."

"I guess," answered Mr. Tidd, "that you're right." His eyes looked sorry—sorry, I guess, to find out anybody was so dishonest. "You're right. I'll go to-morrow—to-morrow."

He did go next day, down to Detroit to see a patent lawyer that Mr. Whiteley told him was all right. Before he went he brought his turbine back to his shop in the barn and put a new padlock on both doors. It was while he was away that the things happened which gave the Ku Klux Klan a chance to show what it was made of.

CHAPTER IX

Next day Mr. Tidd went packing off to Detroit to see the patent lawyer, and we were all at the depot to send him off. So was Mrs. Tidd. She always came to see him off, she said, because if she didn't there was no knowing whether he went or not, or where he went to. Once, she told us, he had started alone to go to a town twenty miles east of where they lived, and two days after she had got a letter from him saying he was in another town thirty miles west and wanted to know what he came there for.

She stood by him while he bought his ticket, and then pinned it inside his coat pocket with the end sticking out a little so the conductor could see it.

"If the end don't show," she said to him, "you'll never find it, and like as not you'll git put off the train. Now when the conductor comes along he can see it and tell you where it is."

Mr. Tidd smiled at her as patient as could be and patted her hand. Then he felt to see that the *Decline and Fall* was in his pocket all right, and smiled again at everybody. He was one of the smilingest men I ever saw, and as soon as you saw him do it you liked him right off, whether you knew him or not.

"I've put a paper in your satchel, right on the top, telling you just what to do. When you git there you pin it on the wall right over the washstand, and don't you dare to go out of the hotel without readin' it. It tells about puttin' on a clean collar, and to be sure not to go traipsin' around without a tie, and such-like. Don't you go neglectin' it, now."

"I won't, my dear, I won't."

The train came snorting in, and Mr. Tidd got aboard all right without forgetting his satchel. We reminded him of it. He sat down in the smoking-car and smiled at us through the windows, and Mrs. Tidd shook her finger at him like she was warning him not to forget anything. Then the bell rang and the conductor hollered "All aboard," and he was gone.

"I'll never draw an easy breath till he's back again" said Mrs. Tidd, and she came close to the truth, for she did draw a lot of uneasy breaths before she saw Mr. Tidd again, and so did the rest of us. In fact, I guess there aren't many folks who have drawn as many uneasy ones as we did for the next several days.

We took Mrs. Tidd home and then looked around for something to do. First we thought we'd go up to see Sammy at the cave, but Mark said he'd gone off up the river fishing and maybe wouldn't be back that night, so we all sat down on Tidd's front fence and whittled and talked and wished something would turn up.

"I guess I could git our horse and rig," Binney said, after a while, "and we could take a ride out into the country if we wanted to."

"That's better'n nothin'," I told him; and the other fellows seemed to agree, so we went off to Binney's house, and his mother, after arguing a while and telling him the horse would run away and break all our necks, finished up by saying we could go. We took the two-seated rig. Plunk and Binney sat in the front seat, and Mark and I got in behind, which made it pretty crowded for me.

"Which way'll we go?" Binney wanted to know.

"Let's go up the river-road," Plunk said. "Maybe we'll meet Sammy somewheres with a string of fish and he'll give us some."

We started off and drove along slow, because Binney's horse couldn't be made to go any faster, past where the cave is and on around the bend of the river where the banks get flatter and flatter until they are a sort of marsh with the river flowing through the middle of it. I guess the road must be a quarter of a mile from the water along there. We must have driven four or five miles, and I know I'd never been so far along this road before. It was like seeing a new country, and we pretended we were explorers and had to keep a lookout for savages and wild animals and such things. Mark was great for that kind of games; and, for a fact, when you got interested in them they were a lot of fun. You could come pretty close to imagining the things really *were* happening that you were *imagining* were happening.

"There's a house," said Mark, pointing. "Looks like the chief lived there. Maybe we can make friends with him; or maybe there's gold piled up there that we can g-git away with."

"There'll be guards hangin' around with bows and arrers and spears," Plunk objected. "They'll up and stick us full of holes before we can wink."

"Seems like I hear one of them savage war-drums a-beatin'," says Binney. "Maybe he's gatherin' together his army to make an ambush for us."

"We better go cautious. Tallow, you sneak ahead like a scout to see we don't run into no trap."

I got out and went slinking along by the side of the road, keeping hidden as much as I could in the bushes. After a minute I passed an orchard and came to an evergreen hedge. I poked up my head, cautious-like, and looked over. I never saw a yard with so many evergreens in it, all trimmed in funny shapes and sticking up everywhere. They were so close together you couldn't see anything of the house but the roof. I watched quite a spell, but I couldn't see anybody moving, so I sneaked back and reported that we weren't being watched.

Mark called a council of war, and we decided to go ahead in a body, the real object being to get a drink of water, but we made believe we were after the chief's gold. Just like Indians we wormed and squirmed along to the hedge and poked our way through where a bush had died out. It was a close squeeze for Mark, and he got scratched up considerable, but he got through just the same. Right off we began prowling around among all those evergreens, getting closer and closer to the house. We were all so interested in the game we clean forgot about the water and everything else.

At last we were crouching behind two bushes not more than ten feet from the steps. Mark raised his hand and pointed around one side of the house, motioning for Plunk and Binney to reconnoiter that way while he and I would go the other way. At that we rushed sudden from our cover to the corners of the house and went spying around, peeking in the windows, looking for savages or signs of the gold. At one window in the wing Mark stopped and looked careful. He waited for me to come along and pointed. I peeked in and saw that the room was all fixed up for somebody to do mechanical drawing. There were the same kind of tables and drawing boards and instruments the engineer had who built the city waterworks in Wicksville. But everything was new, you could see that, and hadn't ever been used.

"Funny thing to be in a chief's wigwam," I whispered, and he nodded. He sat down with his back against the foundation and with his chin in his hands, the way he always does when he wants to figure out something he doesn't understand. I could see he was puzzled about the drawing things way out there in that farmhouse, and if I left him alone he'd sit there maybe an hour trying to fit sort of an answer to it.

"Come on," I whispered. "No tellin' when these savages'll come rampagin' back. Let's git out of this."

So he came along until we met Binney and Plunk. They hadn't seen a sign of life, and it was pretty clear the chief was off on some sort of expedition; but we were worried because there wasn't even a little lump of gold to be seen through any of the windows—not a smidgin!

"Maybe he's got a secret hidin'-place."

"Prob'ly with some horrible image a-stand-in' guard over it," Binney said, and shivered like he was a little chilly. "They always have them awful-lookin' images with grinnin' mouths and maybe seventeen arms and legs a-guardin' their secret and sacred places." He'd got so interested that he could almost see a whopping big carving of some scary thing standing right there in front of him.

"Most likely we'll have to find a hidden spring to touch. There'll be a huge stone stuck against the openin'."

I was getting tired of talking about it so much, so I up and said: "Well, let's git to lookin' for the place. We can study how to bust into it when we find where it is."

We started off toward the back of the yard, when all at once Mark halted us and pointed off to the left. "Th-there it is!" he hissed. "The cave! Up that precipice! See the openin'?"

We looked and, sure enough, we saw what Mark meant. It was the icehouse with a little square opening up near the very top and a ladder nailed to the wall running up to it.

"It ain't guarded," says Binney, his mouth open like he was surprised most to death.

"How in the world did they ever come to neglect that?"

"The guard's there," Mark says, contemptuous-like. "Don't you see him a-stand-in', leanin' on his spear? We got to hide around the corner and git him before he gives the a-a-alarm."

We hid and waited for the guard to come along, and then we pounced out on him, and I guess he'd have been a pretty surprised guard if there'd been one at all. We knocked him down, and Mark sat on him and held his mouth shut while the rest of us tied him up tight. When he was taken care of Mark says, "Now for the treasure!" and commenced climbing up the ladder.

We all followed and scrambled through the little door in on top of the sawdust that the ice was packed in to keep it from melting during the summer. It was almost dark in there, and just like a great cavern.

"It's g-g-gold!" shouts Mark, picking up a handful of sawdust and letting it run through his fingers. "Millions and millions of dollars worth of it. We're rich men." He said it just like some fellers we read about in a story of hidden treasure did. When they found *theirs* they got all excited and said lots of things like that, and Mark was always for doing things the way the books said.

I crawled over to the door to look down the precipice and see if our guard was still tied up all right, and I tell you I jerked in my head quick, for there was a man standing right at the foot of the ladder looking up, and he had the biggest dog with him I ever saw.

"Fellers," I whispered, and I was scared, all right, "the guard's got loose, and he's waitin' for us to come down with a trained lion to help him."

They thought I was still playing, and partly I was, but the man was there, all right, as they saw when they looked. Pretty soon we knew he'd seen us, for he hollered, and his voice sounded old and mean and squeaky. "I got ye, all right, consarn ye. Come sneakin' and spyin' around a feller's house, will you? I'll learn ye what's what 'fore I git shut of ye." He waited a minute, then he spoke to the dog. "Watch, Obed, watch!" I thought that was a funny name for a dog. "Git 'em if they come down." And then he went off leaving that whopper of a dog sitting right under us where he could gobble us if we came down.

"FELLERS, THE GUARD'S GOT LOOSE, AND HE'S WAITIN' FOR US TO COME DOWN"

"Well!" says Plunk, like somebody had poked him between wind and water.

"Well!"

We all crowded to the little door and looked down at the dog. He was lying with his muzzle between his paws, and it looked like he was all ready to go to sleep.

"Don't look like he amounted to much as a watcher," said Binney. "I bet we could walk right past him."

"Wait till he's fast asleep and try," Mark said, and kind of grinned.

We waited maybe fifteen minutes, and I can tell you it was beginning to get pretty chilly in there with all that ice and gold that had gone and turned back into damp sawdust. We were getting more game than we had figured on.

"Don't see what the man was so—riled about," Plunk grumbled. "We hadn't done nothing to him."

"Thought we come to coon somethin', I guess," I told him; and that seemed likely, but when we got all through with the man and the house we knew that wasn't the reason at all.

"I'm a-goin' to try," says Binney, and he shoved his legs through the door and begins crawling down the ladder. He was about halfway down when the dog grunted and cocked his ears and sat up on his haunches and looked at Binney with his big eyes. Then he yawned, and we could see right down into his red throat, and every tooth in his head stared at us and we stared at them. Binney began to climb back again, and never said a word when he was through the door and sitting on the sawdust once more.

"Better watch-dog than you c-c-calc'lated," says Mark, slyly-like, with his face as sober as Deacon Barns's when he asks for offerings for the heathen.

Nobody thought of anything to say, and we kept getting chillier and chillier and uncomfortabler and uncomfortabler. Binney was uneasiest of all, because there was his father's horse and rig standing by the side of the road, and no telling when somebody'd come along and borrow it, or something would come along and scare the creature till he ran off. It was a nice pickle to be in, any way you looked at it, and when the way you looked was toward that dog it was prettier than ever.

"We got to git out," I said.

"S-s-sure," Mark chattered. "Show us how and we'll come right along."

But that wasn't so easy. It began to look as though we would have to stay and take our medicine—whatever medicine the mean-looking, wizened-up old man intended to give us a dose of.

CHAPTER X

Mark crawled over to the little door and peered around. He pushed both his fat legs through and sat with his feet dangling, and I saw him begin to pinch his cheek between his thumb and finger.

"There," I says to the other fellows. "He's got to work now. Just you wait, and Marcus Aurelius Fortunatus Tidd'll fix up some sort of scheme to make that dog wish he was off in the woods barkin' at a woodchuck."

Pretty soon Mark began to drag in his legs, which was considerable of a job, and his little eyes were twinkling, though the rest of his face was solemn and without any more expression than a round apple dumpling, which it looked like a whole lot.

"Fellers," he says, "have you got a slingshot among you?"

Both Binney Jenks and I had, and good full pockets of bully round stones, too.

"Good," says Mark. "We'll give Mister Man a s-s-seance."

"A what?"

"A s-seance—that's a sort of ghost party, where spooks go prancin' around. Wonder if he's s-superstitious."

"He looked like he was right mean, if that's any help," says Plunk.

"Where you goin' to git your ghosts?" I was curious to find out.

"These here'll be sling-shot ghosts."

"G'wan!" I sneered; but I was pretty sure he'd hit on some scheme better than ordinary.

"What's the scary part to the ghost stories you know?" he asks.

I thought it over, remembering all the hair-raising stories I ever heard—sort of telling them over to myself to see what was the part that made them creepy. Well, sir, you'd be surprised, but it was the same thing in every one of them—noises. That was it—noises—mysterious noises that you couldn't see any reason for. It didn't matter what the noise was, just so there wasn't anything around to make it. It could be a door squeaking or a chair moving or a footstep or a cat miauing or anything. I told Mark.

He nodded three times. "Sure—noises. Well, we're goin' to give this feller noises—mysterious noises."

"How?"

"Sling-shots. See that dinner-bell?" He pointed to an old dinner-bell hanging on the pole back of the house.

We could see it, all right, but we couldn't see what good it was going to do.

"Can you h-hit it with your sling-shot?"

I took a good stone and fitted it in the leather, then I knelt close to the door and took aim careful as I could. They waited, holding their breaths until I let go the rubbers, and in a second the old bell said *glang* just as plain as if somebody had rung it. Mark grinned until all the fat on his face looked as if it was trying to climb back of his ears. "Fine," he says; "now keep away from the door."

"Why?"

"So he won't see us and think we done it. It's got to be mysterious, ain't it?"

We got a little back from the door, and I shot again, but this time I missed. Binney took a try at it, and *glang* went the old bell.

"Wait," said Mark.

Pretty soon we saw the old man come poking out of the house and look around. He walked back to the bell and looked up at it and turned all around, watching everywhere, but of course there wasn't a thing to be seen. When his back was to the bell Mark said to shoot again. I let her go, and *glang* went the bell. The old man jumped like I'd shot him instead of the bell, and looked up at it with his eyes sticking out big as eggs. I'll bet it was a mighty mysterious happening to him.

"*N-now*," says Mark, "shoot the d-dog."

I scrouged close to the door and let the old whopper have one in the ribs. He jumped worse than the old man did when the bell rang and said "Yip, yip!"

Well, there was another noise for him. He came walking our way cautious, and he was as pale as a pond-lily. When he was about half-way I let fly at the bell again, and when it *glanged* I thought he was going to throw a fit. He wheeled around to look that way, and Binney reached out quick and gave the dog another. He yowled again, and around came the old man, but there wasn't a thing to see. We could sit back where he couldn't see us and plug away at his bell all day. We rang it twice, one *glang* right after another. If I'd been that fellow I calculate I'd most have jumped out of my skin, just as he did. What with the bell a-ringing without anybody to ring it, and the dog a-yelping without anybody to make him yelp, it was spooky enough to suit anybody, and a lot more than enough to suit *him*. You could see he wished there was five or six other men with him, or that he was off in the next state.

"Hey, up there!" he yelled, with his voice trembling and squeaky. "Hey!"

We never said a word; just kept as still as though we weren't there at all; and I guess that helped. It always is sort of creepy to call somebody you're sure is right there and not hear a sound. You get to wondering what's happened to them, and—well, you know that kind of cold and wrinkly feeling you get just at the back of your neck. And to top it off we gave the old bell another lick. He turned and made tracks for the house.

Well, we weren't helped much so far. "Give it to the dog," says Mark; and we did, twice, good and hard. He set up an awful yelping and the man began to run, but he stopped and began whistling and calling. The dog went running after him, pretty glad to get away, I guess. I had it figured out the old man wanted some kind of company and wanted it bad, so he'd rather have the dog with him than watching us. He went hustling up to the back door, and just as he opened it Binney whanged the bell again. Well, Mister Man just waited to let in his dog and slammed the door shut so hard he 'most broke its window; and on top of everything I banged a stone right against the panel. I'll bet he thought the ghost was rapping for him sure.

"He don't come out again for a week," says Plunk; and it did look as though he'd holed himself in for quite a stay.

"Guess we can git down now," says Mark.

We climbed down the ladder cautious and sneaked out through the evergreens and behind the hedge, keeping out of sight of the house till we got to the road. Nobody made a move after us.

"Wonder who lives here?" Mark was always curious.

"Look on the mail-box," I told him; "the name'll be there."

He crawled along to the little tin box on the post in front of the gate. The name was Harvey Willis. None of us thought anything of that then, but it wasn't very long before Mark did think something of it by putting two and two together. He was great for doing that. Give him a couple of facts, and he was the greatest fellow that ever was for taking them and reasoning all sorts of other facts out of them. I never saw his beat.

Binney's old horse was standing just where we left him, and I thought he looked kind of disappointed to see us come back. Most probably he'd been having a horse-dream about standing right there in the shade forever with lots of fresh green grass to eat and no work to do. Seeing us, and Mark Tidd in special, must have been quite a shock to him. I'd sort of hate to have to pull Mark around myself.

We got into the rig and started for home, stirred up quite a bit and excited over our adventure. It was Mark that began showing us his pockets full of sawdust. Said he'd had presence of mind enough to get a cargo of gold even when we was being besieged and fighting for our lives against awful odds. The rest of us were sorry *we* hadn't got some treasure, too.

"The old Ku Klux Klan showed it was worth somethin' that time," says Binney; and we all agreed with him.

Mark told us about a lot of famous escapes out of history, and we sized them up and compared them with ours; and if we hadn't been about as smart as any of them, then I don't know what I'm talking about! Ours was as good a scheme as any Mark had to tell about.

We drove along, making believe we were pursued and that the horse was galloping madly, which was a kind of a joke, because that animal couldn't have gone fast enough to break the law on the sign over the bridge about riding or driving across faster than a walk. We stood ready with our sling-shots to sell our lives dear, and, considering everything, we were having as much fun as I've had for a long time.

We kept looking along the river-bank hoping to catch sight of Sammy, but he must have gone farther up, because we didn't see any trace of him. There was no telling how far he had gone; ten or fifteen miles wasn't anything to him at all, and sometimes he'd be away as much as a week. When he came back he'd tell us about hunting or fishing in a lake or woods maybe fifty miles off. I never saw his beat for walking—all day and all night he could keep it up without getting tired, and as for getting lost or wondering which was the right way to go, why, it never bothered him at all. He was like one of those pigeons that carry letters; take him where you wanted to and he always knew the way to start for home.

Maybe we had gone a mile when we saw a cloud of dust ahead that had a horse and buggy in the middle of it driving faster than farmers usually do when they're coming home from town. At first we thought maybe it was the doctor on a hurry call but the horse wasn't gray, so we knew it couldn't be him. In a few minutes the rig was close enough so we could see the man driving, and I like to have fallen out of our carriage, for it was nobody in the world but that Henry C. Batten who was sneaking around the engine-room the day before. There he was, as big as life, and we thought sure he had gone back to Pittsburg. He went by in a flash without even looking at us.

"Well," I said to Mark, "what d'you think of that?"

"I think," said Mark, frowning a little, "that we're goin' to have to keep our eyes open. If that feller's hangin' around after dad's turbine, now's when he'll try to git it—with dad away."

"Jinks!" he says in a minute, slapping his knee. "That name on that post-box was Willis. He's drivin' that way. The engineer's name was Willis—in Mr. Whiteley's place, I mean—and he's in cahoots with this Batten. Fellers, he's a goin' to that place we just left."

It sounded likely, the way Mark reasoned it out.

"Well," says Plunk, "what are we goin' to do about it?"

"Nothin'," Mark says, "but wait and keep our eyes open."

It was a pretty serious business, we thought, with Mr. Tidd away and nobody to depend on but just the Ku Klux Klan. Still, considering what we had done off and on, we believed we were pretty well able to look after things in a pinch.

We hurried up Binney's horse and got home in plenty of time for supper. In the evening I went over to Mark's, and we put in the time putting a brand-new padlock on the shed where the turbine and the drawings and things were. That made us feel safer. So when it got too dark to play around outside we went in and fussed with a lot of stuff Mark had and looked at books. Along about half-past eight Mrs. Tidd brought in a big plate with fried cakes and apples and hunks of maple sugar on it, and we attended to that the way it ought to be attended to. Afterward I went home.

I went to bed and fell asleep right off. I got to dreaming, and it seemed like somebody was whistling the Ku Klux Klan whistle to me and I was tied up so I couldn't come or even speak—one of those funny kind of dreams when you feel as though you couldn't even wink, and yet can't figure out what it is keeps you so still. And all through it I kept hearing the whistle and straining and trying to get up, but it wasn't any use. After a while it seemed as if somebody was trying to blow me up with dynamite or something. There came an awful crash in the dream, and I woke up standing in the middle of the floor. I was shivering and scared so my teeth chattered. Then I heard the Ku Klux Klan whistle again, and something came smack against my window. I guess that was the explosion I heard in my dream. I stuck my head out and there stood Mark Tidd, looking as big as all get out, with the moon shining down onto him as white as silver.

"What's the matter?" I called to him.

"Q-q-quick!" he says. "Come down. Somebody's busted into the shed and s-s-stole dad's t-t-turbine." He was so excited he stuttered like anything.

"G'wan!" I says.

"It's gone," says he.

"What time is it?"

"'Most one."

Well, it was the first time I ever did it. I didn't like to go sneaking off without telling my folks, but I judged the circumstances kind of demanded something special, so I got into my clothes and slid out on the porch. It wasn't any trick to get down the trellis to the ground. It was cold, and my teeth chattered.

"What we goin' to do now?" I asked.

He didn't say a word, but just set off walking away into the dark, and I followed after.

CHAPTER XI

One o'clock in the morning is a creepy time, even if the moon is shining, and it's a good sight more creepy when you know something has happened. I hurried up to walk beside Mark because it was lonesome behind. He was heading straight for his house.

"Is it gone?" I asked. "Are you sure?"

"The padlock's pried off, and the turbine ain't in the shed."

"How'd you come to find out about it at this time of night?"

"They waked me up. I ran to the window just in time to see 'em drive off l-l-licketty split. Then I went down, and the turbine was gone."

"And then you came after me." I was kind of tickled to think he did that. It showed he depended on me like and thought I'd stick by him and help out. "Did you see who it was?"

"No."

"Which way did they drive?"

He jerked his thumb down the street. "No tellin' which way they went. Prob'ly turned the corner; I don't know which way."

He went around through his yard to the workshop, and, sure enough, the padlocks had been pried off and Mr. Tidd's engine was gone. I didn't quite realize it till then, and I tell you it struck me all in a heap. There was Mr. Tidd off in Detroit, seeing about his patent and confident of getting rich, and here we were, left to look after the engine, and we'd let it get away from us.

"Maybe he can get his patent anyhow," I said; but there wasn't much comfort in that, for Mark explained that it couldn't be done. His father had to have a model that would work, or no patent would be given to him. He was sure that Henry C. Batten was at the bottom of it all, and so was I.

"What they're goin' to do," he said, "is to take dad's turbine and make draw-in's from it. They'll git another model made and smouge the patent before we kin b-begin to put a new one together."

"They won't dare take it to the depot and send it on the train," I told him.

"Not from here. Maybe they'll drive to some town near by and p-put it in a box and send it that way."

"Maybe," I says; but somehow I didn't think so. Neither did Mark, I guess.

"Let's see if we kin follow the wagon tracks," he said, and got a lantern out of the shop.

It wouldn't be so hard to do at that time of the night, because there weren't any other wagons driving around, and the wheels of this one would be the last wherever it went. Besides, it had rained a little earlier in the night, and the dust in the roads was pasty.

We followed the tracks down the alley a couple of blocks; then they turned, and Mark muttered that he thought so.

"Thought what?" I said.

"That they'd turn this way—toward the river."

"Why?"

"Because," he said, "that's where the Willis farm is."

He told me as we walked along what he'd reasoned out. From the minute the turbine had been taken he began thinking and thinking the way he always does and putting two and two together. At last he got it into his head that he knew where the men were taking his father's engine. First, there was Henry C. Batten driving on the road toward the Willis farm; second, Willis was the father to the engineer who had sneaked Batten in to see if the turbine worked; third, old Mr. Willis acted more skittish than ordinary when we came around, and, says Mark, that showed he had a guilty conscience; and last, and what Mark called the clincher of the whole thing, was that room in the farmhouse all fixed up with drawing-tools and tables just waiting for somebody to come in and set to work. I thought it over, and it looked to me as though he'd argued it out pretty straight.

"I guess," I says, "the place to look for the engine is out at Willis's."

We followed the wagon tracks quite a ways farther just to make sure, and then turned back for home. It was beginning to get kind of pink in the east when I scrambled up to my room again and rolled into bed. I'd promised Mark to meet him early in the morning to see what we'd do.

I went over to his house right after breakfast, and he was at the gate waiting for me. "Careful what you say," he told me. "Mother don't know, and there ain't no use frightenin' her yet."

"All right," I says; "now what's your scheme."

"We can't do nothin' till we *know* where the turbine is and who t-t-took it. We think we know, but we got to make sure."

"Let's git at it, then," I says. "What'll we do—walk? It's five miles."

"I don't want Binney and Plunk along—there'd be too many of us, and we might get caught, so we can't git Binney's horse."

All of a sudden an idea hit me. The river ran right by the Willis house, and I owned a kind of a boat, flat-bottomed, but not very heavy. It was one of the kind that sort of skims over the top of the water without setting down into it much, and it was easy to row.

"What's the matter with my boat?" I says.

"Say, that's the very thing."

"And I got two pairs of oars," I told him, and most laughed out loud. Marcus Aurelius Fortunatus Tidd never cared much about exerting himself to speak of, and the idea of rowing a boat five or six miles wasn't one he cottoned to worth a cent. He was sorry about the other pair of oars, and he showed it; but he didn't say anything, and I knew he'd row the best he knew how when he got in the boat. If he had to work he'd work, and there wouldn't be any soldiering. If he could get somebody else, by some scheme or other, to do his work for him he'd be tickled to death, but just to come out and loaf like some fellows do—well, he wouldn't do it.

I kept my old boat above the dam tied up to a stake back of my uncle's saw-mill, and in ten minutes we had pushed her out into the river and were pulling up-stream, taking it easy so as not to tire ourselves all out at the start. It took us half an hour to get to Brigg's Island. Above that the current got swifter, and we were quite a spell getting to the little island across from our cave. We went up the outside branch because the water was so shallow on our side, but we could see a little smoke going up from the place where the cave was, so we knew Sammy was home again. It's lucky he was.

We rowed a little farther and then pushed in to the bank to rest a bit.

"We want to land a little this side of Willis's," Mark decided, "and s-s-sneak up same as we did the other day along the fence."

"'Tain't likely they'd hurt us."

"I dunno. Never can tell when men are doin' things like this. But I wasn't fig-gerin' on gittin' hurt, only on bein' seen. If they found somebody was s-s-spyin' on 'em they'd up and s-s-scoot. Specially if Batten was to see me. I ain't easy to forgit." Mark grinned when he said that. He was right, though; Batten might not remember me if he did see me prowling around, and he might think I was just a kid playing some game or hunting or something; but if he caught sight of Mark, why, he'd know who it was in a minute and why he was there.

When we were rested up we got into my boat again and up the river we went. We rowed and rowed and rowed. "Thank goodness," I said, "it won't be such hard pullin' comin' back. We kin float down with the current."

In about another hour we came to the island in the bend of the river, a quarter of a mile below Willis's. Here the river ran through a big marsh that stretched, all green with tall water-grasses and cat-tails, on either side, and there wasn't a good place to land. We didn't want to have to wallow through the marsh, because we knew we'd get in mire up to our knees and maybe higher, and because it looked just like the kind of a place where rattlesnakes would be fussing around. In general, I'm not afraid of rattlesnakes, but I don't like to go plunging through a place like that and maybe stepping right on one before he has a chance to rattle at you.

Back among the reeds and grasses we could see lots of muskrat houses, and we stowed that fact away to remember, because you can make pretty good money trapping rats and selling their skins; and I thought it would be a fine place for wild duck in the early spring.

We turned back a little to where the shore was more solid and found a place where a rail fence ran right down to the water. We made for that and tied the boat. It wasn't much of a trick to clamber along the rails to shore, though Mark made them bend so I thought it wouldn't be very surprising if they broke. That fence wasn't built to hold fat boys, but to keep in cows.

There was a bank maybe ten feet high to climb before we got to the road. We looked up and down pretty careful before we got up in sight; but nobody was coming, so we ducked cross to the north side where there were a lot of hazel bushes growing along the roadside, and some blackberry bushes, as we discovered by the prickers when we pushed our way through them.

We were pretty cautious, keeping back in the bushes and ready to lie down out of sight if anybody came along, but nobody did, and so we got to the old orchard that was next to Willis's house. It was a pretty big orchard, but it hadn't been looked after very well, and the grass was high. The limbs of the trees came close to the ground, and, take it altogether, it made a pretty good place to sneak through if you didn't want anybody to see you coming.

It was easy enough to get up to the rail fence that went down that side of Willis's yard to the barn; and it was safe enough, for the fence corners were full of bushes and big weeds where we could have stayed as long as we wanted to without anybody seeing us. We didn't come to hide in a fence corner, though.

"Well," I says, "we're here."

"We're on the wrong side of the house. What I want to do is get a p-p-peek into that room where the drawin' things were."

"We kin go around."

"We got to," says he.

"Hold on!" I says. "There ain't no need for both of us to go trampin' all over the place. One kin see as good as two, and if I am seen it won't be so bad as if you were. You stay here, and I'll go crawlin' around and see if I can't get a shot at that window. I bet I can get there all right."

He thought a minute, sort of hesitating, because Mark wasn't the kind of a fellow to let somebody run a risk he ought to run; but he saw it was the best scheme to let me go, so he nodded. "Maybe I'll find somethin' to do here," he says. "Be careful."

I went crouching along to the road, intending to go past the house under cover of the hedge that ran across in front of it. I was halfway across, I expect, before I thought of the dog. Now, I've found out that it is pretty easy to get around without a man seeing you; but it's quite another thing to be so still a dog can't *hear* you, and I never found anybody who could stop a good watch-dog from *smelling* him. But, dog or no dog, I had to look into that room, for, if Mark had guessed right, there's where his father's turbine would be, and nowhere else. The drawing-man would want it there to take his measurements from and to see how it went together.

I ducked past the gate as quick as I could, though there wasn't really any need, for there were so many evergreen trees growing around in the yard that you couldn't see the gate from the house, anyway. I've seen a lot of farmhouses with six or seven evergreens growing in their front yards for ornaments, but I never saw anybody who seemed to like them so well as Mr. Willis. There were more than a dozen of them, set in rows, and all trimmed and pruned into funny shapes like balls and cones and one thing and another. I was glad he did like them; it came in mighty handy for me.

There was a field of corn on the side of the house I was heading for, and it wasn't very far up, not far enough to hide in; but there were quite a few clumps of bushes along the fence, like there always are on farms where the men that run them are shiftless. I got behind one of these and took a good look at everything to see how the land lay and to make up my mind just what to do so as to get a look through that window.

The house was about a hundred feet away, and between me and it was a fairly large maple tree. Back at my right, a little nearer the fence than the house, was the icehouse where we got caught the day before. From where I was I could see the dinner-bell that had helped us out. Back of that a little was the woodshed, and way at the far corner of the lot was the barn and the corn-crib. There was smoke coming out of the kitchen chimney, but nobody was out in the yard or anywhere in sight.

I figured it out that the thing for me to do would be to run across the yard as fast as I could, look in the window and dash back again over the fence. If I was quick enough nobody'd see me, and it wouldn't give the dog a chance to smell me either. So I threw my leg over the top rail and let myself down inside. Then I sprinted toward the big tree which was between me and the window I wanted to look into. I wasn't more than halfway to the tree before I heard the front door open, and somebody came out on the porch. I couldn't see them yet, but I daren't take any chances of their coming around into the side yard where I was. I just jumped for the tree and grabbed the lower limb. It didn't take me a second to swing myself up among the branches, and the leaves were so thick that I knew I was safe if that dog didn't come nosing around.

I felt in my pocket for my sling-shot, thinking maybe if the dog did come I could fix it so he wouldn't want to stay where I was very bad. By luck the sling-shot was there and a couple of dozen good pebbles. I tell you I was pretty thankful.

It was lucky I went up the tree, for I heard steps coming toward my end of the front porch, and then there stood Henry C. Batten in his shirt-sleeves, smoking a big cigar.

He stepped down off the porch and whistled. I didn't like that whistle a bit, because it meant I'd have the dog sniffing around that part of the place, and I'd much rather he'd stay where he was. But he came galloping up from the barn, and Henry C. Batten stood there and patted his head and scratched his back. Then he picked up a stick and threw it right my way for the dog to fetch. Over he came, licketty split, but I guess he was so busy with his game that he didn't notice me. The man kept him running back and forth quite a while till he got tired of it; then he and the dog began to stroll around the yard. They walked all around until they came to my tree, and then what did Henry C. Batten do but sit right down on the grass in the shade and light another cigar, as if he was going to stay there the rest of the afternoon.

I would have given my jack-knife to have been anywhere else but right there. The leaves were good and thick, and the chances were against Batten seeing me, but, all the same, he might see me, or the dog might smell me, and then where would I be?

I kept pretty still, you can bet, and held my breath so that wouldn't make any sound. It was all right for a little while, but just you sit all doubled up in the crotch of a tree without moving even a finger and see how long you like it. I got a cramp in my leg, and my back ached, and my arms got tired. I never was so uncomfortable in my life. The cramp in my leg kept getting worse and worse, and there isn't anything I know of that hurts so much as a good big cramp just above the knee. I thought I'd have to holler right out. Finally I couldn't stand it any more. I *had* to straighten out that leg and get rid of the cramp—that was all there was to it, I *had* to. So I did. It made a little rustle in the leaves, and my heart came up in my mouth so I could have bit it. Henry C. Batten looked up, but, thank goodness, he couldn't see me. The dog looked up, too, and began to walk around the tree and sniff. It was just what I had been afraid of all the time. Then he began to bark.

"What's up there, old fellow?" Henry C. Batten says. "Is it a bird?"

The dog kept on barking. Batten got up and looked around for a stick. When he found one he stepped off a piece and threw it up into the tree, and out flew a big bird with a lot of fuss and flutter. I never was so much obliged to a bird in my life.

"There he goes," says Batten to the dog; and then he walked off toward the house again. But the dog kept on hanging around my tree. Batten turned and whistled to him, and after a couple of times he went along, but even then he kept looking back and growling. It's a wonder Batten didn't suspect something.

I watched them turn out into the road and walk down past the orchard.

"Well," I said to myself, "it's now or never." So I dropped down out of the tree and ran to the house. I could see in the window by getting on tiptoe, and I didn't lose a second doing it. There was the room, drawing-tables and tools and all, and right in the middle of the floor was what I came to discover—there stood the Tidd turbine!

I didn't wait a jiffy more than necessary, and anybody that had tried to race me back to the fence would have had to go pretty fast to come in even second. I don't know how I got over—half fell and half jumped, I guess—but, anyhow, I got over, and there I was safe and sound, but shaking all over as if I had a chill.

It took me maybe twenty minutes to get back to where Mark Tidd was waiting. He was sitting with his back against the fence and an old piece of paper spread on his knee, drawing something.

"Well," I says, "here I am—and it's there."

He seemed pleased like to think he'd been right in all his surmises, and nod-ded.

"What you doin'?" I asked.

"Makin' a map," says he. "I've been prowlin' around, and here's the lay of the land. It'll be a handy thing when we come to p-p-plannin' how to git the engine away."

"Which," says I, "don't look like sich an easy job as some I've heard of."

He stuffed his map in his pocket, and when we saw Henry C. Batten and the dog come back from their walk we hustled down to our boat and rowed home. It was late in the afternoon when we got there and I was most starved—I'd hate to have had to feed Mark—for we hadn't had anything since breakfast.

That night Mark drew out his map all in ink, showing everything, and you'll find it here if you're interested in the lay of the land around the Willis farm.

CHAPTER XII

It's lucky the schools had been closed for two weeks on account of a diphtheria scare, for it's hard to see how we could have got along if it hadn't been that way. We had a whole week before us yet, and if we couldn't get back Mr. Tidd's turbine in seven days we couldn't get it back at all. But we didn't lose any time just because we had a little of it on hand. Mark Tidd was no time-loser.

Next morning he got me out of bed 'most as early as if it was the Fourth of July, and lugged me off down to my boat.

"We hain't a-goin' to row all the way up there again, I hope," I says, because there were blisters on my hands, and my back was stiff, and, anyhow, rowing ten miles or so is a joke I don't like to have played on me every day hand-running.

"We'll just row as far as the c-c-cave," Mark says. "Then we'll git Sammy to row the rest of the way."

"Oh," says I, "Sammy. What good'll Sammy be, *I'd* like to know. Might as well fetch along the Perkinses' Jersey calf."

"Sammy kin lift," says Mark. "How'd you figger we was goin' to git the turbine out of the house? Whistle to it and have it follow us like a d-d-dog?"

I didn't have anything more to say. I might have known he wouldn't take Sammy without some good reason.

"It's quite a heft even for Sammy," I told him.

"He's *got* to carry it."

We rowed up the river again and landed near the cave. Sammy was there, all right, because his fire was smoldering, so we climbed up the hill and hollered at him. He came sticking his big head out of the opening and grinned at us like he was tickled to death to see us, which most likely he was, and says, "Nice fish — bass. So big. Sammy fry in pan, quick. Sammy good cook."

"We ain't got time to eat to-day, Sammy," I told him; and he looked as disappointed as a baby that didn't get the candy somebody promised it.

"We got to go up the river in my boat," I says, quick, "and we want you to come along."

He grinned again, and all his teeth showed as white as polished pebbles. "Catch fish, maybe, eh? Good boys, big friends to poor Sammy. Sammy show where to catch fish — big fish."

"Not to catch fish this time. You tell him, Mark."

"We want you to help us, Sammy. Some men have taken father's engine, and we got to git it back. They're b-b-bad men, Sammy, and they might hurt us. And there's a dog."

He grinned wider than ever. "Sammy take dog—so." He showed us with his big hands how he'd grab the dog and throw it far enough to bust its neck—and I bet he could have done it, too. "Bad men take engine, eh? Um! Sammy git it back. No 'fraid of bad men. Sammy big, very big. Bad men afraid of Sammy, eh? Sammy scare bad men so they keel over flipflop."

I thought likely Batten might keel over flipflop if he met Sammy on a dark night, and somehow it made me feel better about the whole thing. Sammy *was* big. Why, it would have taken all of Batten and Willis and half of the dog to make another like him—and then Sammy could have licked the fellow they went to make up.

"Got boat?" he asked.

We pointed down to the river, and he nodded. "Sammy git ready. Fetch pan to cook, and fish-lines. Maybe stay long, eh? Maybe git hungry. Good boys feed Sammy—now Sammy feed good boys—maybe, eh?"

He put a couple of pans and a bundle of other stuff into the boat, and then without our hinting at it at all he took the oars; and the way he sent that boat skimming up-stream made me ashamed of the way Mark and I had gone the day before. He seemed to take it easy, too, like it wasn't work at all, but play.

We got to the little island—maybe there was a couple of acres in it, all told—and Sammy stopped rowing a minute. "Bad," he said, pointing to it and scowling. "Very bad little island. Boys keep off—always. Don't never go on island."

"What's the matter with it?" I wanted to know.

"Snakes, big snakes! Lay in deep grass and go *k-r-r-r-r-r* with tails." He imitated a rattler so I 'most jumped out of the boat. It sounded as if one was right there under my legs all ready to strike.

"Oh, rattlesnakes."

He nodded two or three times. "Heaps, many. Bad place. And snakes not all—poison ivy. Boys, stay away."

"You bet we will," says Mark.

The island didn't look like much of a place to land, anyhow, snakes or no snakes. It was low, with more bushes than trees on it, though there were quite a few butternuts and some whopping willows. It looked marshy and soggy, and I calculated we could get our feet wet most anywhere except, perhaps, right in the middle, where the butternuts were thickest.

Mark showed Sammy where to land over by the old rail fence, and when we got ashore Mark drew out his map that he'd made the night before and showed it to us. Sammy looked at it with his eyes bulging out like blue robin's eggs—only bigger.

"Fat boy make map, eh? He make river, house, barn, trees?"

Mark admitted it, and it didn't take half an eye to see he was pretty proud of his work. Sam patted him on the back and grinned like he thought the map was wonderful and Mark was wonderful, too, and *that* didn't make Marcus Aurelius Fortunatus Tidd feel small or mean. He never minded being admired a bit.

"It's a good map, all right," I says, impatient-like, because it wasn't any fun squatting down there in the muck, "but how's it going to help us git back the engine?"

"Tallow," says Mark, looking at me like he was sorry to see such ignorance in anybody, "we *got* to have a map. How we goin' to plan our campaign without? Tell me that. This is like a battle," says he, "and battles is planned out ahead with m-m-maps."

"Maybe so," says I, "but if I was general of this army I'd be stirrin' around Willis's, I would. I guess I know the way around there pretty well without any map."

"Well," he says, disgusted as could be, "come on, then."

He folded the map and stuffed it in his pocket. I started to climb the bank first and was half-way up before Mark or Sammy were on their feet at all. I wasn't cautious about it like I ought to have been, and went sticking my head right up in sight without ever spying around to see if everything was safe and clear. It served me right. I stuck my head over the top of the bank, and was hauling the rest of my body after, when I looked up, and there, looking at me kind of surprised, stood Henry C. Batten.

"Well," says he, "where'd you come from?"

I was struck all in a heap, but I knew I had to do something to keep Mark and Sammy from popping into sight and to keep Batten from walking over to look down where they were. I reckon I looked scared. But I took hold of myself and sort of whispered in my own ear that now was the time to do some quick thinking and quick acting. I grinned at Batten. It's always a good plan to grin when you can't think of anything else. Folks like to be grinned at. I grinned like I was tickled to death to see him, and says, "Have you heard any frogs a-hollering around here?"

I didn't wait for him to answer, but jumped up in the road and walked across to him. I didn't want him coming over to me and looking down the bank.

"Frogs," says he, "I should say I had heard some. That marsh is alive with 'em."

"I ain't been able to git near one in a mile," says I. "I kin git a nickel a dozen for them down to the hotel."

"How d'you get 'em?" he wanted to know.

"Whallop 'em with a club. I got to git a new one, too. A longer one with a knob on the end of it. Guess I can cut one off 'n that hick'ry yonder."

There was a big hickory about a hundred feet off, and I started for it, and of course he came following along. It's a funny thing, but folks always will follow like that. Just meet a man or a boy or a woman and point to something and say you're going to do something or other to it, and he'll come mogging along as interested as if you were a balloon ascension.

"Gimme a boost up," I says.

He helped me and I got hold of the lower limb and was up in a minute. It was a smooth-bark hickory, and good clubs were growing all over it. It was a regular club tree. I got out my knife and began sawing away at a limb. It was hard cutting, but I got it off pretty soon and dropped it down on the ground. I came down after it, and trimmed it up, talking to Henry C. Batten all the time.

"Summer boarder?" I asked him, looking at his clothes.

He grinned. "Well, something like that," he admitted. "I guess, seeing the time of year it is, that I'm a *spring* boarder."

I laughed fit to split. There ain't a better way of getting on the blind side of a man than to 'most laugh yourself sick when he makes a joke. I did my duty nobly, if I do say it myself, and it wasn't much of a joke to laugh at, either.

"Who you spring-boardin' with?" I snickered; and then I made a sort of joke of my own. "That sounds like you was stoppin' at a swimmin'-hole, don't it? Spring-boardin'?"

He laughed, and after that I wasn't worrying much. If ever you get in a tight place with a man just laugh at something funny *he* says and make him laugh at something funny *you* say, and the worry's over. Somehow you can't get to suspecting a fellow you've been laughing with.

"Where d'you live?" he asked me.

I jerked my thumb over my shoulder. "Back there a piece," I said, which was true, all right. But it was *quite* a piece—five miles or more.

When I was done trimming my frog club I shut my jack-knife and, when Batten wasn't looking, dropped it on the ground near the tree where I knew I could find it again. Then we started to walk up the road toward Willis's.

We walked along quite a ways until we'd got so far I judged Mark and Sammy would have had time to get well out of sight. Then I began feeling around in my pockets and looked worried. "I dropped my jack-knife somewheres," I told him. "I bet it was under that tree."

I felt through my pockets some more, but of course it wasn't there. "I'm goin' back," I says. "That was a new knife, and I can't afford to lose it."

"No, I s'pose not," he says. "Well, good-by. If you get any frogs bring 'em to me at the next house. I'll pay you ten cents a dozen for good ones."

I didn't wait, but started running back as if I was anxious about my knife. I *was* anxious, all right, but the knife hadn't anything to do with it. By the time I got to the tree Batten was out of sight around the bend of the road, so I went right to the bank and looked over. Mark and Sammy were gone. I whistled the Ku Klux Klan whistle, and got an answer from out toward the river where Sammy and Mark had pulled the boat and hidden it in the reeds. As soon as they saw me they knew it was safe, and came pulling in to the rail fence again.

"Whe-e-ew!" I called, "but that was a close shave."

Mark didn't answer anything, but after he and Sammy were up in the road he said, "I been thinkin', and what we got to do f-f-first is git rid of the dog."

"It would be a good thing to do, all right, but he don't look to me like an easy dog to git rid of."

"You wait," says Mark, and winked at Sammy. The big fellow grinned and pulled a whopping bass out from behind him.

"Maybe dog like fish, eh? Maybe he come to git fish. Then Sammy catch him, so. Dogs like Sammy—never hurt Sammy."

"Maybe," I said; "but this don't look like a friendly dog."

Sammy only grinned.

We sneaked up toward Willis's through the bushes and hid in the orchard like we did before. There wasn't anything to do but wait, so we waited. The dog wasn't in sight anywhere. We sat there maybe an hour, when Mister Dog came stretching and yawning out of the barn and walked through the yard to the front gate. Sammy, still grinning all over his great, round face, crept on all fours along the rail fence and got out in the road. We stayed where we were because we couldn't help any that we could see, and, anyhow, the idea of fooling with that dog didn't hold out any inducements. I got a grip on my club and made up my mind that if he did sail into Sammy I'd help all I could; but, thank goodness, it wasn't necessary. In no time at all we saw Sammy, with a rope around the dog's neck, waiting for us at the fence.

"Nice dog," says he, when we came up. "Like fish very much. Give him lots of fish, maybe, eh? Now what we do?"

"We'll tie him up," says Mark. "Lead him down the road far enough so he can't be heard barkin'."

We marched him a quarter of a mile off and tied him a rod or so back from the road in the woods.

"There," I told him, and gave him a pat on the head, "I feel better with you here. You're a weight off my mind, and no mistake."

"Now," says Mark, "we'll git down to business."

He had things planned out, all but the getting of the turbine. It looked to me like that was the important thing, but it didn't seem to bother him very much—sort of took it for granted we'd get it out of the house, all right, but he was worried about how we'd get away to Wicksville with it and without getting caught. He said the first thing to do was to take my boat up the river to Willis's and run it up through the marsh. I guess somebody there liked to fish or row or something, for they had dug out a sort of canal from the river through the marshy ground and right up to the solid bank. There was a flight of rickety steps leading up the bank, and at the bottom was a little square landing-place. What we had to do, Mark said, was to get the boat to that landing, or near enough to reach, and keep it there without letting anybody see it till Sammy came down the steps with the engine in his arms.

It sounded easy enough to get the boat there and hide it, but I couldn't see, for the life of me, how we were going to get into the house and haul out a big machine without having somebody catch on.

"It's always the hardest part," says Mark, "that's easiest done. It's because you try harder. The great schemes that have failed did it because somebody got m-m-mixed on a little thing." And he told us a lot of instances out of history and stories. It looked like he had the best of the argument, but that didn't get the engine into the boat.

CHAPTER XIII

We waited until we thought everybody in the house would be eating dinner, and then we rowed up the shore and turned into the Willis's cut. Nobody saw us, but we didn't breathe easy till we were under the high bank and sheltered from the house. Of course, we weren't safe even then, for if anybody had looked down there and seen a strange boat tied alongside the scow of Mr. Willis's he naturally would wonder about it and want to know who came in it and where they were. Sammy fixed that part of it up pretty well by shoving the boat out a dozen feet and then throwing a big armful of brush over the bow of it. He ran the rope through the grass and left the end where we could get at it in a hurry and haul the boat in. I went up as far as I dared on the steps, and everything looked safe to me. Unless you were suspicious and looking for something you wouldn't have noticed the boat at all.

"Tallow," says Mark, who had been sitting on the bottom step pinching his cheek, "folks that're scairt are easier to f-f-fool than folks that ain't."

"I guess so," says I.

"They're worryin' about themselves, and wonderin' if anything's goin' to hurt 'em, and when a feller gits to fussin' about himself he ain't got much t-t-t-time to think about anything else."

My, how he spluttered!

"That's right," I says, remembering well how I'd felt that night at the cave keeping watch all alone and wondering what had made the footprint in the sand with the toes off to one side. "Scare a man good and you got him."

"What scares a man most—somethin' he kin see or somethin' he can't?"

I saw what he was driving at right off. "Why, somethin' he can't see and can't understand. The more mysterious it is the more scairt he'll git."

He nodded. "Then," says he, "the thing for us to do is scare Batten and the rest of them stiff."

I knew by the looks of him that he had a scheme; you could always tell by the winking of his eyes and the way he wiggled his left thumb sort of excited-like.

"Go ahead," says I; "let's have it."

"We started it the other day with the dinner-bell. I bet old Willis is shiverin' about that yet. We kin give 'em some more of it. Then, maybe, Sammy kin help us. Remember his showin' us how a p-p-panther screamed?"

I should say I did remember. I never heard such a blood-curdling noise in all my life. I was sitting right by Sammy at the cave when he made it, and it was broad daylight, but the little hairs on the back of my neck rose straight up, and I was nervous all the rest of the day. I should say I *did* remember it.

"We'll use that, and then they'll be discoverin' the disappearance of the d-d-dog. If other things has happened *that'll* bother 'em some. Maybe, too, we kin fix it so they'll see Sammy's footprint. Oh, I guess we kin s-s-scare 'em, all right."

I began to think so, too.

"Let's commence," I says.

"You go around into the orchard and whang at the bell. Sammy and I'll stay on the east side and see what we kin do. When I give the whistle make for the boat."

I made for the orchard and crouched down in a fence corner where I could get a good sight at the bell. I'd filled my pockets chock full of the best stones I could find, nice round fellows about the size of marbles, and there were new rubbers on my sling-shot. I hadn't taken any chances. When I was all settled I got to my knees and let her fly. The first time I missed, but the second time the old bell went *glang*. I scrouged down out of sight and waited. In a minute old Mr. Willis stuck his head out of the door, his eyes bulging, and looked all over. He stood there quite awhile, sort of undecided. Then he turned his back, and at that I shot again. *Glang* went the bell, and he jumped a foot. When he landed he was turned all the way around.

"Hey! Mr. Batten! Mr. Batten!" he yelled.

Batten came running to the door to know what was the matter. Willis was excited and talked loud, so I could hear every word he said. He started in by telling how the bell rang the other day with nobody to ring it, and how the dog had yelped, and how something had slammed the door when he went in. "It ain't nat'ral," he squeaked. "I dunno what's doin' it, but it ain't the hand of man. No, siree! And here she's just rung twice right under my nose."

"JUST RUNG TWICE RIGHT UNDER MY NOSE"

"Bosh!" says Batten. "You're nervous and dreaming."

"Didn't you hear that there bell ring?"

"I was in the front of the house working; I didn't notice anything."

They were facing each other and not looking toward the bell at all, so I let her have another one. *Glang* she went, and I thought Willis was going to fall off the steps. "There!" he yelled, shaking his skinny hand in Batten's face. "There, maybe you heard that, eh? Maybe I was dreaming then. Now, tell me what made that. Who rung it? No human bein' rung it, I say. Something's gone wrong with this place, it has! It's ghosts, that's what it is; and I'm a-goin' to pack and git for town."

"Ghosts!" snorts Batten. "Bosh!" But he didn't look easy in his mind, and was watching the bell uncomfortable-like. "There ain't no such thing," he says.

"No sich thing! Why, my father he—"

He'd got Batten looking at him instead of the bell, so I banged it again. This time Batten jumped most as high as Willis.

"Bill!" he yelled; "come here, Bill!"

A big young fellow in his shirt-sleeves, with a pencil in his hand, came to the door. I judged he was the drawing-man that was taking off the design of the engine. They palavered quite a spell, and I didn't get a chance to shoot; besides, I didn't want it to get too common. Even a ghost that hangs around too much will get to be a habit; folks will get used to it, and it won't scare them any more. I let them talk.

"Where's the dog?" says Batten, all of a sudden, and commenced to whistle and call. Of course the dog didn't come, and you could see *that* worried them.

"He never goes off," said Willis, and he tried whistling; but the dog was a long ways away, and the rope that tied him to his tree was good and stout.

"This," says Batten, "is getting to look kind of funny." He was one of those middle-sized men with too much under their vests, and a sticky-looking complexion, and eyes that always seemed as if somebody'd just spilled a mite of water into them. He wasn't handsome at any time, but now he got kind of yellow mixed with green, and his fingers began to shut and open. By all signs he was pretty average uncomfortable.

Well, just then Sammy let out an awful screech like a panther that's been shot. It went up high and came down low and went into your ear like it was trying to bore a hole through your head. I'd been expecting it, and I knew what it was, but that didn't make a bit of difference; I was about as scared as Batten and Willis. They got white; I could see it way where I was. The color seemed just to pop out of their faces. It seemed like I ought to have heard it make a noise like when you pull a cork out of a bottle.

"What's that?" says Batten, and grabs a hold on Willis.

Willis he didn't say a word, but just sagged against the door, and the fellow they called Bill ducked inside and then poked his head out and glared all around with his eyes almost laying on his cheeks. I took another crack at the bell.

Every one of them jumped into the house and slammed the door. I didn't think it would be a good idea to do anything more just then, but to sort of let what we had done sink in. So I sat still, watching the house. All at once I heard a sound close behind me, and, being pretty excited anyhow and all on edge, I liked to have jumped up and hollered, but I didn't, which was lucky, for it wasn't anybody but Sammy, grinning away and plumb tickled to death with himself. He motioned with his finger for me to follow him.

"Fat boy says come," he whispered, and then giggled. "They jump, eh? *Ding* goes bell; they jump. *Ding* goes bell; they jump some more. Sammy laugh and fat boy laugh. Then Sammy make panther screech. So. Everybody jump. I guess bad men scairt, eh?"

"They looked scared to me," I says. "But scared is as scared does. Wait till we see."

We all laid up among the trees a couple of fields east of Willis's and had some sandwiches and one thing and another which I had been wanting quite a while. It was way past noon, and I hate to have meal-time go by without paying some kind of attention to it. After we ate we took it easy. Sammy went to sleep and Mark dozed. I never can do much sleeping when it's daytime—seems like such a waste of time—so I started cutting my initials into a big elm tree. While I was whittling I got to thinking; I guess there isn't a better way to think than to whittle. Just get your knife going good, and your head seems to go at the same time. I bet if I could whittle all the time in school I'd stand up at the head of the class. Things don't puzzle you so. You just sit and think, lazy-like, and the first thing you know you see it just as plain. Well, I began figuring out what we were doing without intending to think about it at all, and all of a sudden we began to look pretty foolish to me. Yes, sir. Mark and I looked foolish, and Sammy was foolish, anyhow, so there we were. I reached over and kicked Mark.

"Wake up!" says I.

"What's m-m-matter?"

"I been thinkin'."

"That ain't no reason for wakin' me up."

"This is a silly thing we're a-doin'," I says.

That made him sit up sudden, for if there was anything he hated it was to look silly, or to do anything foolish and get caught at it. I don't know what he wouldn't have done to keep folks from laughing at him, or from getting into a scrape that made him look ridiculous.

"What's silly about it?"

"The hull thing," says I, "from A to Izzard."

He puckered up his face and his eyes got squinty, like they always do when he's mad. "If you want to back out," he snaps, "go ahead."

"I don't look like backin' out, do I?"

"What's the matter, then?"

"Oh," says I, "the hull idee of it. Ain't it sort of reedic'lous for you and me, a couple of kids, and Sammy, a half-witted Injun, comin' up here to git the best of three growed men, and one of 'em from Pittsburg? Why," says I, "them men forgit more from breakfast till dinner than all of us know put together."

"Maybe so," says he.

"They were smart enough to git your pa's engine, and I bet they're smart enough to keep it, leastways so far as us kids is concerned. Seems to me we went at it wrong. Hadn't there ought to be some way of gittin' back that engine without smougin' it this way? I bet there is. What we should 'a' done was to go to some man in Wicksville we could trust and find out what to do."

He didn't say anything, but looked like he'd lost his last friend. Anybody could see I was right, and he couldn't do anything else but admit it, but admitting wasn't one of the things Marcus Aurelius Fortunatus Tidd hankered to do oftener than was necessary.

"And," says I, "so far's scarin' 'em goes, what good'll it do? Maybe we kin keep old Willis hoppin', and maybe we kin make Batten and the other feller a little nervous, but with *them* it ain't goin' to last. They're city men, and eddicated men, and when they git to thinkin' it over they're goin' to be more mad than scairt, and they'll be lookin' to see who's puttin' up a job on 'em. Ghosts is all right for old codgers like Willis, but you got to trot out a perty lively sperret to keep Henry C. Batten a-guessin' long."

While I was talking Mark was cocking his ear up the road, and I stopped to listen. Faint-like we could hear a rattling, and a tinny sort of sound, with a whistle going high over it all, a whistle that was whistling "Marching Through Georgia" with bird warbles and jumps and trills and things all scattered through. It kept coming closer and closer and louder and louder. We crept out and looked up the road. It was a horse and wagon, a big wooden wagon, painted the kind of red that railroads paint their box-cars; and it looked pretty much like a little box-car for a horse to draw. There wasn't anything funny about it, for that kind of wagons came through Wicksville half a dozen times a year. It was a tin peddler who traded dish-pans and stuff like that for old rags and rubber and what-not. Sometimes they'd have a big bundle of buggy whips besides the tinware.

The driver was lopping back on his seat, with his nose pointed straight up, whistling away like he was paid for it by the hour. You couldn't see much of his face but the under side of his chin, which isn't rightly face at all, I suppose. When he got opposite us I began whistling "Marching Through Georgia," too, as loud as I could. He brought his head down slow and sat up, never missing a note. Then he jerked on the lines to stop the horse and looked down at us, his face all puck-ered up with his whistling, and went right on until he got to the end of the verse. He was an oldish fellow, with one of those long, thin faces, sort of caved in at the cheeks, that usually go with lean six-footers. His skin was wrinkled and brown, and his eyes, which had a lot of wrinkles running every which way from them, were brown, too. His hair wasn't red, and it wasn't yellow, and it wasn't any other color I ever heard of. He quit whistling, as I said, when he got to the end of the verse; but he didn't speak right off, only looked at us and felt of his nose, wiggling it a little with his fingers like he wanted to make sure it was on right and wasn't likely to go flying off unexpected. Then he spoke with a voice that was little and squeaky and raspy.

"My name," says he, "is Zadok Biggs. I venture to say you never heard that name before—Zadok. No? It is rare, very rare. It was given to me in a spirit of prophesy, of prophesy by my father, a remarkable man. Zadok, my friends, is from the Hebrew, and signifies Just. You see! Just Biggs is my name, then—and it fits. Nobody can deny that it fits. Just by name and just by nature. To that I may add just by habit and just in dealings. I have a judicial mind, my friends and who knows, had not commerce lured me from my books, but I might have risen to greatness in the law—even to the bench of the Supreme Court in Washington? Who can say?"

None of us could, so we kept still about it.

He kept right on. "Ah, you look pleasant, and you listen well. I will dismount—climb down is the commoner expression—and rest with you."

He got down clumsily and when he stood on the ground we saw that he wasn't five feet high, but almost three feet wide. You looked at his face, and felt sure it belonged to a man six foot six long by a foot wide and skinny; then you looked at the rest of him and—well, he didn't match. He'd got hold of the wrong head somewhere.

His horse edged over and began eating grass.

"There," said Mr. Zadok Biggs, "is a lesson for you, my friends. Take it to heart. Learn from dumb creatures, learn from nature, learn from man, learn from books, learn everywhere and anywhere. The lesson my horse teaches at this moment is: Neglect no opportunity. You observe he eats. He might well have stood in the sand without eating, but, behold! the opportunity to eat presents itself, and without hesitation he avails himself of it. Bear this in mind—never overlook opportunity."

"We're around here lookin' for opportunities, but there don't any seem to show up," I says. And Mark scowled at me to keep still.

"Don't be discouraged. I don't know what kind of an opportunity you want, but, whatever it may be, it will come. It always does. Everything has got an opportunity tied to its tail like a tin can, and if you keep on listening you'll hear it jangling."

I could see that idea pleased Mark, and he began to look more cheerful.

"What did you say your names were?" asked Mr. Biggs. "Not Wilkins, I hope, nor Sauer, nor yet Perkins. I can't abide those names, so give me warning if any of them are yours and I'll be going on. I can't have anything to do with a man if he has one of those names."

"Mine's Martin," I told him, "and that's Marcus Aurelius Fortunatus Tidd, and that over there is Sammy—just Sammy."

"Very good, very good, indeed, especially our friend here to the right. His parents have displayed marked aptitude for naming children. His name is an achievement, a mark of genius. I should like to grasp the hand of the parent who gave you that name."

"It was my father," says Mark. "He got it out of the *Decline and F-f-fall of the Roman Empire*."

"Excellent! You have made me your friend for life. Bear it in mind. I, Zadok Biggs, am your friend for life. Your name did it; I shall treasure it in my memory. It stands at the top of the list—the very top."

He talked on and on, telling us about his travels and adventures, asking us a question once in a while; and altogether I thought he was a pretty good sort of a man, and better company I never met. At last he says: "You were speaking of opportunity. May I inquire—ask is the more common word—what opportunity you are looking for. I do not desire to pry. Zadok Biggs is the least inquisitive of men, but perhaps I can aid—help—you with my advice."

"We are lookin'," says Mark, and I was mighty surprised at him, "for an opportunity to git back a t-t-turbine."

"Oh," says Zadok Biggs, looking kind of blank and bewildered, "a turbine, eh? Of course, a turbine—engine is the more usual expression, I believe. Who, if I may ask, has the turbine?"

Mark told him the whole thing, and he nodded his head and muttered and scowled as he listened. When Mark was done Zadok Biggs sat still a long time. Finally he said, "There are no two ways about it, the opportunity would come, but, I pause to ask, will it come soon enough, or if it comes will you be able to take full advantage of it. On these points I must admit, in spite of your name, that I do not know. It seems dubious—doubtful is the more customary expression—very dubious." He stopped again and pulled two stalks of grass which he chewed and chewed like he was getting some sort of help from them. Pretty soon he says, "If I were you, in your circumstances and surroundings, I would go back to Wicksville, a fine town, and tell the story to a man I could trust. It would be the safer way, the surer way. Mind I do not say your schemes are impossible—nothing is impossible to a boy named Marcus Aurelius Fortunatus Tidd, nothing, but it would be safer."

Mark frowned and looked at the ground. After a while he raised his eyes and sighed. "If," says he, "the opportunity ain't showed up in an hour I'll go b-b-back."

Zadok Biggs scrambled to his feet and clambered up on his wagon. "I'm journeying—driving is the more usual word—to Wicksville. I shall arrive to-morrow, for I stop to-night on the way. Bear in mind that I am your friend—your friend for life. If I can be of assistance—do anything for you—let me know. I shall be easy to find."

With that he drove off down the road, whistling "Marching Through Georgia" to the top of his voice, or to the top of his whistle, and we watched him till his wagon turned the bend.

"Well," says Mark, "he seemed to agree with you."

"Yes," I says. "He's a man of good sense."

"B-b-but I got an hour yet," Mark says, getting in the last word.

CHAPTER XIV

Pretty soon we couldn't even hear the tin-peddler's whistle, and Mark got up onto his feet, painful-like. He stretched, which was taking a chance on busting out some seams, and yawned. Lots of things Mark Tidd does look funny, but if there's anything more comical a fat boy can do than yawn I'd give something to see it.

"Just an hour," says he, "to f-find that opportunity."

"Might not take ten minutes," I says. "From what I know of opportunities they're onreliable. They're just as apt to catch you early in the mornin' as late at night. No tellin' when they come prowlin' around."

"We'll go ahead like I p-planned for an hour. Then we'll go home if nothin' hasn't turned up."

"Good!" says I. "That suits me down to the ground."

"There ain't but sixty minutes in an hour," says he, "and every one that gits away from you is one less you got. Let's be stirrin' around."

"Stir ahead," I told him, getting onto my feet. "Get your old spoon to workin'."

Mark was looking at Sammy with a kind of glint in his eye. He didn't need to tell me he was thinking of some use to put that big fellow to; you could see it sticking out all over him.

"Um," says he. "You're too dangerous-lookin' to waste, Sammy."

Sammy grinned like it was the finest compliment a boy could think of, and wriggled his toes. Well, sir, that was all Mark needed to give him an idea—just the wiggling of a toe.

"That's the ticket," he says in his tickled-to-death voice. "Wasn't there a fresh-spaded flower-bed just in front of the porch there, Tallow?"

"All raked over and as neat as a pin," I says. "Bet the seeds hain't been planted six hours."

"It's where they'll be s-s-sure to see it."

"Right under anybody's nose that comes out on the porch."

"Fine! We'll give 'em somethin' to look at, then. Now, Sammy, listen to what I'm a-goin' to say to you, and listen good. You jest make believe all of you is Injun and that you're a-crawlin' up on a camp of enemies. The camp of enemies is the house, and if you git seen they'll more'n likely burn you at the stake. Well, you go mouchin' along till you git to that flower-bed, and then you up and step careful right in the middle of it with that b-b-busted foot of yours. Leave a good, plain mark like was in the sand at the cave. Then come back a-kitin'."

Sammy grinned some more and wriggled his hands and sort of twisted all over like a cat does when it wants you to feed it. We watched him crawl down along the hedge, and then all at once he ducked out of sight, and, no matter how we strained our eyes, we couldn't catch even a wabble of the bushes.

"If it looks as mysterious to Batten as it did to us I guess they'll do considerable wonderin' about it," I says.

We sat pretty anxious and quiet waiting for Sammy to come back. It didn't look to us like the folks in the house could do Sammy harm once he got a start, but somebody might come onto him unexpected and swat him with something; and then where'd we be, with nobody to carry the turbine if we did manage to get a hold on it? But we needn't have worried. The first thing we knew there was Sammy standing right by us, chuckling like all get out.

"Sammy step on flower-bed. Sammy careful—oh, very careful. Make foot show plain. Make Sammy's funny foot show in dirt. Sammy helps, eh? Big help?"

"You b-bet Sammy's a help," Mark told him, and patted him on the back. "We never'd git anywheres without you, would we, Tallow?"

"I should say not," I says, just as solemn as I could; and maybe you think Sammy wasn't tickled. Why, he most wiggled out of his skin!

"I'm goin' to sneak over and see if anything happens," says I. "I kin hide among the evergreens and watch. It ought to be worth seein'."

"Don't go takin' no r-r-risks." Mark like to have strangled over the last word. "Keep your ears open, and if I whistle the whistle, come a-runnin'."

I went around in front and wriggled through the hedge. Nobody was in sight around the house, so I squirmed up, dodging from tree to tree until I was only about twenty feet away from the steps. There I crouched down among the prickles of a fat evergreen and waited. I could see the steps as plain as could be, but you'd have had to hunt for me careful to have found me, even if you knew I was hiding around.

Well, it wasn't more than ten minutes before Bill came out rubbing his hand like he'd been writing or drawing and the muscles were tired. He sat down on the top step and pulled a cigar out of his vest. I could see the red-and-gold band around it. He bit off the end and struck a match. I was interested to see how he snapped the match away, and made up my mind to try it myself. He shot it just like I'd shoot a marble, and it went straight. It fell right on Willis's flower-bed. Now, when you snap a thing that way you always watch to see if you hit what you shot at, or, anyhow, to see where you do hit, and Bill saw the match strike right alongside of Sammy's footprint. I saw him lean forward quick and stretch his neck. He grabbed a hold on the post and pulled himself up, and then walked over to the bed. He leaned over, knelt down, and I could hear him grunt with surprise.

"Well," says he to himself, "well."

In a minute he got up and went into the house. Before long he came back with

Batten, and both of them looked at the footprint.

"What is it?" says Bill.

Batten looked kind of funny and shook his head.

"Look at them toes," Bill says, after a while. "Look at 'em, growin' right out of the side of the foot. No man ever made that," says he.

"Too big," Batten agreed, shaking his head some more.

"There's only one footprint. I looked," Bill says. "It hasn't made a mark anywhere else around. I don't like it, not me. Feet with toes off to the side and bells ringin' without anybody to ring 'em. I tell you I don't like it."

"Shucks!" Batten snorted.

"Well, what made it, then? Looks as if it didn't have but one leg and come down out of the air just to make a footprint. I wish we was a good ways away from here."

"So do I, but not on account of the bells or the tracks in the dirt."

"I never took any stock in ghosts, but that track makes me shiver—and them bells ringin'. And old Willis is so scairt he can't eat."

"Come on," Batten says, sort of savage, "let's skirmish around the yard and see if we can't see what's doing it all."

"Batten, you can skirmish all you want to, but not for me. I ain't hankerin' to meet the thing that made that mark, not me."

"Shucks!" Batten growled again. "Get a club and come on."

That sounded fine to me, I can tell you. Get a club and come on! I was afraid enough of them without clubs, so I waited just long enough to let them turn their backs, and off I was. I couldn't get out of the yard, though, before they were back, and each of them had a cane big enough to knock a horse down with. They didn't separate—seemed like both of them wanted company—but they did begin poking all over the front yard. Every chance I got I edged away farther, and I managed to keep a bush between the men and me all the time. At last I had to take a chance of being seen or else get caught, for they had me cornered, so I watched for the best time, and up and dived through the hedge like I was jumping off a spring-board. I landed all in a heap outside.

"What's that?" Batten says, sharp.

"Somethin' went slam through the hedge—somethin' heavy."

You can just be sure I didn't wait. I picked myself up and skedaddled, keeping close to the bushes, and was safe and sound before they got up courage to look over at the place I dived through.

"They're consid'rable stirred up," I says to Mark, when I got back. "You ought to have seen Batten and Bill look at that track."

"Did it s-s-scare 'em?" He was excited as could be.

"Scare 'em! Huh, I bet they won't go to bed in the dark for a month. Let's not give 'em any rest. Jest keep whangin' away at 'em all the time that's left to us."

"Well, then, git over where you were behind the fence, and we'll give 'em some more ghost-ringin'."

I went crawling back, and got into my fence corner all right. I'd been so lucky getting one place and another without being seen that I was feeling pretty well satisfied with myself and figuring that I was about as good, maybe, as Leatherstocking and a lot of those old fellows that have been written about so much. Which shows that it's bad luck to get to liking yourself. I never knew it to do any good, and nine times out of ten it upsets your apple-cart.

I peeked up through the bushes, and there, not more than fifty feet off, sat Henry C. Batten and the big young man he called Bill smoking and taking it easy in the shade of a little apple tree. I sat quiet and listened to them talking.

"The funny thing," says Batten, "is where that dog has gone to. That's what's bothering me."

"Gone off chasing a rabbit."

"I s'pose a rabbit rang the bell, too, huh? And let out that screech. I ain't denying it's got on my nerves, and Willis is ready to crawl under the bed. 'Tain't ghosts, I know that—when I get time to think it over—but it's all-fired queer. I'd give something to know how that bell was rang and who rung it."

I just couldn't resist the temptation to let her fly. My sling-shot was all ready with a pebble in it, and I hit the old bell a good clip. *Glang* it went.

Batten and Bill sat up straight. Maybe they were sure ghosts hadn't anything to do with it, but they didn't like it. They got up and walked over by the shed where they could look up at the bell.

"There isn't any string tied to the clapper," says Batten. "I thought it might be a black thread—some kid trick. If it is a kid I'd like to catch him a minute." He looked good and mad and a little frightened, which is a bad combination. I said to myself I'd be in for a good mauling if he did catch me.

I was having too much fun, though, to quit, so I let her have another one. This time I hit it sort of glancing on the side, and it rang, all right, but the pebble went bouncing off and whanged against the side of the shed not a yard from Batten, and fell almost at his feet. He couldn't help seeing it.

"Well," says I to myself, "you've gone and spilled the beans now." And I had, too. Batten stooped over and picked up the pebble and then looked around to see where it could have come from. It didn't take more than a cabbage-head to puzzle that out, for I was in about the only place where a fellow could hide and shoot at the bell—outside of the icehouse. Batten didn't wait for anything, but came running right at the fence, and Bill was at his heels.

I didn't wait.

The orchard was behind me, and I turned, letting out a holler, and was off through it, running faster than I ever ran before. Batten and Bill had to climb the fence, which gave me a good start, and the trees kept them from getting a good sight of me. I made for the road, which was foolish, but when a fellow's frightened he's likely to do foolish things. You see, I wanted to get where I could run faster, and didn't stop to think that the men who were after me would be able to run faster, too. I should have kept to the fields and the woods. A heavy man can't get over the ground when it's rough and bumpy like a boy can.

Batten wasted quite a bit of breath yelling at me, and so did Bill. I guess between them they made racket enough to stir up a good slice of that side of the country. But they were better at yelling than they were at running, and even in the road, where things were easier for them, I kept all of my lead, and even gained some. But they stuck to it. I suppose both of them were pretty mad. There aren't many things, I've noticed, make a grown-up man so mad as to be scared good without any reason, especially if the scaring has been done by a boy. They chased me clean to the bend of the river, and then all at once I heard old Willis letting out screeches and hollers from the house.

Batten stopped as quick as a wink, and Bill stopped, too. I slackened down some myself and listened. Whatever could have happened to the old man I couldn't figure out, but he was sure enough excited, bawling Batten's name and things I couldn't make out and hollering "Help!"

Well, sir, those two men forgot all about me. They turned around and hit for the house. I kept right on going, because I studied it out that Mark and Sammy had been up to something and, whatever it was, it was too late for me to help; and, mad as Batten was, I didn't think that neighborhood was a very good one for me to be hanging around. It was five miles to town almost, but I set out to walk it.

As I went along I got to thinking about the dog that had been tied up now for three or four hours, and I was sorry for him. "I might as well let him loose," I says to myself; "he can't do any harm now."

He was tied up just around the next bend. When I turned it there was Zadok Biggs's red wagon, but Zadok wasn't on top of it. The horse was taking advantage of his opportunity again. I says to myself that if the peddler stopped very often and gave the horse many more opportunities he'd eat so much he couldn't walk, and then Zadok would have an opportunity to doctor him.

I came up close and called. Zadok answered from back among the trees, and I found him petting the dog and feeding him sandwiches.

He didn't seem a bit surprised to see me, but went on feeding the dog, and the dog wriggled around and worked his tail back and forth so hard it rocked his hind legs.

"He likes sandwiches," says Zadok Biggs. "That is an interesting fact. Always make a note of interesting facts. They may some day be of advantage to you—come in handy is the general way of saying it. You see, if you owned a dog like this and had nothing to feed him but sandwiches, you, with this fact in your possession, would not hesitate to give them to him. You would know he liked them. Very interesting and very useful."

"I'm going to let him go," says I.

He nodded. "Where is your companion—Marcus Aurelius Fortunatus Tidd? A name to admire!"

"Back there somewheres, in some kind of a mess, I guess."

"You've been running," he said, and eyed me a minute. "What for?"

"I was being chased."

"A very good reason, very good, indeed. I know of no better reason for running than that you are being pursued—chased, as you say. Who chased you?"

"Batten and Bill," I says.

He began to hop up and down on his short legs; his eyes got bright and he slapped his leg. "Did they chase you far? Away from the house?"

"Quarter of a mile, maybe."

"What made 'em stop?"

"Old Willis was hollerin' his head off back at the farm."

"Opportunity!" says Zadok Biggs, and he danced a little jig. "You never know when it's coming. Never! How does it feel to be an opportunity?" he shot at me sudden-like, "or, at least, part of one?"

"I dunno."

"Martin, I believe your name was? Well, Martin, you have been part of an opportunity for your friend Marcus Aurelius Fortunatus Tidd. The point is—did he avail himself of it? I think! I consider him in the light of acquaintance, and I say to myself, 'Zadok, a boy whose name is Marcus Aurelius would not neglect an opportunity.' If you add the fact that Fortunatus also is part of his name the matter becomes certain. I am reassured—relieved, or made easy in my mind are simpler ways of stating it—Marcus *has* seized the opportunity. You will see."

I didn't know what he was talking about, but he seemed to be all puffed up just like he'd done something wonderful. Mark might have seized an opportunity, but the way things sounded to me it was an opportunity to skedaddle with old Willis screeching after him. I figured it out he'd guess I got away all right and wasn't likely to come back for more, so he and Sammy would take the boat and make for home down the river. The road ran right along the bank, so more than likely they'd be catching up with me before long.

"Martin," says Biggs, "you ain't what I'd call quick; no, not quick, so to speak. I'll tell you what's happened; what your friend Marcus Aurelius has done. He's got the engine, that's what, and he's gettin' away with it this very minute, this identical second."

I saw it all right then, and without so much as saying good-by to Zadok Biggs I went pelting up the road toward the farm. I'd wasted as much as five minutes fussing with the old peddler just when I was being needed, but I ran to make up for it. As I turned the last bend I saw old Willis jumping up and down on the bank, shouting at Batten and Bill, who were leaping down the steps, and a few feet away from the dock was the boat with Mark Tidd and Sammy and the engine in it.

I was most out of breath, but I kept on. When I got pretty close to the cut I jumped over the bank, and, forgetting all about snakes and mud and everything, I wallowed right into the marsh, at the same time bellowing as loud as I could to Mark. The mud wasn't as deep as we'd figured, probably on account of the dirt dredged out of the cut, and I went faster than Sammy could row the boat. I caught them just at the end of the cut and jumped in ker-bang! And there I was.

CHAPTER XV

I have to tell you from hearsay what happened to Mark Tidd and Sammy while I was being chased. I've heard it all so many times I can see it, and if I'm not careful to remember I almost get to believing I was there and taking part in the things that happened.

When I left Mark and Sammy to go around and shoot pebbles at the bell they crept up to the fence on the east side of the house and, Mark says, waited for an opportunity to come along. They heard me whang the bell a couple of times, and then the racket that started when Batten and Bill began chasing me.

"Sammy," says Mark, "run quick and see what's the matter."

Sam ducked around in front and then came running back, all excited. "Men chase Tallow!" he said. "He run! They run! Not catch him, I guess."

They could see old man Willis out behind the house dancing up and down and capering around, but not offering to join in the chase after me. He was pretty nearly over to the opposite fence. The house was all alone.

"Opportunity," says Mark to himself. "He said it would come." Then he turned to Sammy. "Over the fence," he whispered. "Git through that winder and git the engine that's in there. Understand? It's heavy, but you g-g-got to carry it down to the boat. Quick!"

Sammy jumped over the fence and ran to the house, with Mark following as fast as he could. It didn't take any kind of a whack to knock the screen out of the window; and Sammy crawled in, grinning and happy as though he was playing some sort of a game, which I suppose he thought he was.

The engine stood right in the middle of the floor, and he stooped to lift it. First he couldn't get a good hold, but he tipped up one end and got his fingers under, and then got a grip some way with the other hand, and lifted.

Mark says he never saw anything like it in his life. Sammy had a thin kind of a shirt on, and it drew tight across his back and arms so Mark could see the muscles come up in big bunches and knots and rolls. Sammy lifted so hard the muscles seemed like they were going to snap. He bent his knees and got his legs and back into it, and up came the engine from the floor. It seemed like an hour to Mark, but most probably it wasn't a whole minute. Sammy staggered to the window and rested the turbine on the sill. There was just room for him to squeeze by and jump outside while Mark steadied it for him.

"Hurry!" panted Mark. "Hurry!"

Sammy tipped the engine so it slid down into his arms, while Mark grabbed one side so it wouldn't topple over. It was a whopping heavy thing, and Sammy grunted when he got the full weight of it; but he braced himself firmly, using all his strength, and there he was.

"Down to the boat!" stuttered Mark. "Quick!"

Sammy couldn't go very fast with all that turbine to carry, and Mark wasn't much good to help. He was so fat he couldn't get close enough without getting in the way, so he just trotted alongside and held her steady. Sammy panted and puffed and grunted and staggered, but they got along smooth for maybe fifty feet. They were just going to turn in among the evergreen trees, where they would be safe as far as old Willis was concerned, when what should the old man do but come poking around the back of the house!

SAMMY GRUNTED WHEN HE GOT THE FULL WEIGHT OF IT

His eyes lighted on them right off, and he let a holler out of him that 'most split their ears, and stood there shaking his fist and dancing up and down like he was on the end of a rubber. Mark wasn't worried much about him because he knew he wouldn't dare do anything, but he *was* worried about the racket, for it was sure to bring Batten and Bill down onto him. He couldn't do a thing, though, but urged Sammy to hurry, which Sammy did the best he could. It was mighty slow going and seemed a lot slower than it was.

Old Willis followed as close behind as he dared, yelling all the time at the top of his voice; but they got to the top of the bank, and in a couple of minutes they were in the boat and all right. But Mark looked down the road and saw Batten and Bill coming pell-mell, looking as though they meant business. This time neither of the men that had been chasing me bothered about yelling. There was more important business now than catching a kid that had been playing a joke on them, so they saved their breath and put all their attention to getting where they wanted to be as soon as they could.

Sammy started down the steps, and like to have broken his neck, but he managed to keep his feet and make the boat. It is a pretty hard thing to get a heavy machine down easy, and Sammy wasn't used to handling heavy things very much. When he went to lower the turbine it slipped out of his hands and went whang onto the bottom of the boat. They didn't have time to see if any damage was done, though they did hear a board split, but just dug in their oars and started out through the cut. Mark had time and presence of mind to grab one oar out of Willis's boat so they couldn't make very good time chasing them, and off they went.

They weren't more than half-way out of the cut before Batten and Bill were at the foot of the steps bellowing and threatening. Mark said it made him grin to see how mad they were, and how helpless. And right then Mark and Sammy heard me a-yelling to the top of my voice and saw me come plunging into the marsh like I was a regular frog. Batten and Bill tried that, too, but right where they were was a bad hole, and it was so mushy and wet they sank in to their hips and had to go back. I had better luck, like I told you. Then Batten ran off up the steps, and we didn't see him for quite a while, but it turned out he'd gone after another oar.

Sammy had the oars, of course, and he rowed like all get out. We went pretty fast, and the current helped us, but we hadn't got more than what you might call a healthy lead before the nose of Willis's boat came poking out of the cut, and in another minute it was skimming down-stream as fast as Bill could shove it.

When we were almost to the island I felt my feet getting wet, and when I got to investigating I found that there was an inch of water in the boat. When Sammy dropped the turbine it had knocked a hole in her bottom, and she was filling as quickly as a boat could be reasonably expected to, and there we were in a pretty bad pickle. Mark saw it the same time I did.

"Boat's s-s-sinkin', Sammy!" he stuttered. "What we goin' to do?"

Sammy kept right on rowing as fast as he could, and said never a word. "Looks like he's tryin' to think," says Mark, and I guess thinking was more hard work for Sammy than carrying the turbine. But he did it all right—got an idea, and it tickled him so he grinned the widest grin I ever saw on his face.

"We row fast—hide—Sammy know place. Hide boat, hide engine, hide you and me, eh? Good thing. Bad man can't find us. Sammy knows."

I said to myself that it would be mighty lucky for us if Sammy did know, but there wasn't a thing we could do but wait to find out.

The other boat wasn't gaining any; but if our boat should sink, why, there would be an end of the whole thing. And she was getting fuller and fuller every minute. It seemed like an hour before we rounded the head of the island and were out of sight of the men who were chasing us; and then Sammy rowed faster than ever more than half the way to the other end, when, all of a sudden, he turned toward shore and rowed through a mess of weeds and little willows into a sort of bayou, all surrounded by swampy ground, but with a couple of big willows with droopy branches growing right at the edge of the water. Sammy made for one of these and pushed the boat right through the leaves. Mark and I almost hollered, we was so relieved, for back under that tree was plenty of room for the boat, and the growing things were so dense all around that no one could see them from the shore or from the bayou if they found their way in.

"F-f-fine," says Mark; and he patted Sammy on the shoulder.

That tickled Sammy, and he grinned again as wide as before.

But being pleased with the place didn't keep the water from coming through the bottom of the boat, and she was settling and settling. Sammy jumped out up to his knees and grabbed hold of the bow. It wasn't any job at all to haul her up on the mud so she couldn't sink any farther, and that part of it was all right. We noticed that Sammy didn't take any more time about it than was necessary, and scrambled into the boat about as quick as he could. He sat down on the seat and grinned again. "Snakes," he said, "lots of snakes—big. Go k-r-r-r-r." He imitated a rattler as if he'd gone to a rattler school and learned their language.

Mark pulled his feet up and kept them on the seat; partly on account of the water slopping around in the boat, and partly because it made him feel easier in his mind, he said. He never did have any use for snakes—particularly rattlers. For that matter, neither did I.

It wasn't very comfortable, but it was safe. Batten and Bill, most likely, would keep on chasing us down the river, at least for quite a piece. It wouldn't occur to them that we had put in to the island until they got past the lower end of it themselves, and our boat was nowhere in sight. They might come back to look after that, but there didn't seem very much danger of getting found, and more so when you think about the bad name the snakes and poison ivy had given the island.

In about five minutes we heard the sloshing of oars in the river outside, and Batten's boat went splashing past hot-foot—if a boat can go hot-foot, seeing it hasn't any feet, and if it had they'd be in cool water. Sammy chuckled and pointed and showed his big white teeth in the middle of a grin.

"Good place to hide, eh? Bad men go past quick, so. Sammy fool 'em; nobody find Sammy when Sammy hide—no."

"I hope not," Mark told him; "but they ain't begun to miss us yet. Wait till they git around the h-h-head of the island. They'll be comin' back to l-l-look for us then."

"They can't find. Sammy knows. Good place to hide."

For more than an hour we sat in the boat, with muddy water standing a couple of inches deep in it. Mark didn't feel much like talking, and Sammy didn't think of anything to say, and I was scared as all get out. When it was beginning to get dusk we heard the other boat coming slow from up-stream, not down-stream, the way it should have come. It was just moving, and the men were talking. We could hear their voices, but what they said we couldn't make out because it came to us all in a muddle.

They stopped outside the bayou, and we understood Batten when he said: "Looks like there was some sort of a bay in there. See how the weeds and things turn in. Let's poke in there; maybe it's big enough to hide a boat."

Sammy looked at Mark, and he grinned again and winked. He was trying to make Mark feel safe; but it didn't work. Mark didn't feel safe, and I didn't, either, especially when I saw their boat come poking through the high weeds not thirty feet away.

Batten stood up and looked all around. "They ain't there," he said, growling-like. "Where they got to I'd give a dollar to know. Here we rowed all around this confounded island, and not a sight of them. Even if I lost the turbine I'd like to get my hands on that fat kid a minute. He's too smart, he is."

Mark was pretty pleased at that; but, all the same, he didn't hanker to let Batten get hold of him. Compliments are all right, but that kind of a compliment is one you don't get up and bow and say "Thank you" for.

Batten and Bill sat there and rested and grumbled quite a spell, and then, because it was getting dark, they pulled out for home. "Might's well give up," said Bill. "We can't find 'em to-night."

"And we're going to disappear before morning ourselves," said Batten. "We'll keep an eye out for them till the last minute, though."

When they were gone Mark drew a long breath and took time to think about the predicament we were in. It wasn't pretty to think about. There we were, five miles from home by road and I don't know how many by river, with a heavy engine and a smashed boat, and the only land near enough to do any good full of rattlers and poison ivy. How were we ever going to get to the mainland; and if we did, what could we do with Tidd's turbine? Mark never denied that we was up a stump. Anybody would have been.

The only way out of it he could see was to fix the boat and go on down the river that way, but he hadn't anything to fix it with. He didn't even know how badly smashed it was. We could haul it out on shore, of course, and find that out, but a shore like that island made Mark prefer to sit in the boat and figure out some other scheme. Even though it was my boat that was smashed, I felt the same way about it.

"Sammy hungry—Sammy very hungry."

Through the dusk we could see him rubbing his stomach and looking bothered.

"So am I," says Mark, "but I guess I'm goin' to stay that way. We can't eat the b-b-boat."

"Maybe catch fish. Got bait, got line, eh? Fish in river."

"That's all right, but how you goin' to git there to fish for 'em?"

"Sammy dunno. Maybe swim, eh? Maybe git out on island. Maybe git 'em somehow. Sammy very hungry."

"And cold, too, I expect. I know I am. Ugh-h-h!"

"Go 'shore and make fire. Sammy fix so men can't see. Sammy will. Then catch fish, eh?"

"S-s-snakes," said Mark.

"Poison ivy," says I.

"Got to go, anyhow. Maybe snake bite, maybe not; can't tell. Can't fix till we get on shore, eh? Got to fix boat." Sammy seemed to think that when you had to do a thing the only way was to do it; and if rattlers and poison ivy got in the way, why, that was all there was to it—you just had to take what came. It made me feel sort of ashamed of myself to have a half-witted Indian setting a good example like that, and I noticed Mark was looking pretty sheepish.

"Sammy carry boys, eh? Mark pretty heavy, maybe, but Sammy can carry. Tallow he light."

"Sammy'll do nothin' of the kind," says Mark. "I can walk, I guess, if you can."

"Me, too," says I; but I wished I wasn't so proud.

"All right. We go now, eh? Go quick and maybe dodge snake." He grinned like it was a good joke. Maybe dodging rattlers is funny, but I never did anything I felt less like laughing at in my life; and there was the poison ivy, too.

Sammy stepped out of the boat and wallowed toward shore.

"Me n-next," says Mark. "If a snake hits at me he can't m-m-miss."

"Not if he ain't blind," I says, as I followed after.

The way Mark went puffing and plunging like a hippopotamus the rattlers, if there were any around there, must have thought their last day was come. I bet they skedaddled.

Once we got on firm land we never said a word, but made off for the middle of the island, where the big butternut trees were, because we knew we were less likely to run into snakes or poison ivy there. When we got among the trees and stopped, panting for breath, I says:

"I dunno whether I brushed agin any poison ivy, but there didn't no snakes bite me. I heard one, though."

"I heard two," Mark spluttered; "and I heard somethin' a-rustlin' off through the grass. I guess there's more'n a million around here."

Sammy had carried up a little ax and a bundle of other things which he dumped on the ground in front of us.

"Now make fire," says he. "Get warm. Get dry. Trees all round so nobody see. Can't see smoke in dark, eh? Down here good place." He pointed to a little hollow with brush growing all around it and trees along the ridge.

Mark and I didn't feel like moving around much. I had heard a rattler won't bother you if you don't bother him, and nobody has any idea that poison ivy will sneak up and nip you while you're standing quiet. Sammy didn't seem to be worried, though, for he hustled around gathering dry wood. But before he started out I noticed he got him a good big club.

We were tired, but we didn't sit down. We could have sat down, but we didn't want to; we might have sat on a snake. Now, if a rattler is going to bite you I can't see what difference it makes whether he does it when you're on your feet or lying on your back, but I s'pose it's natural to feel safer on your feet.

Pretty soon Sammy had the fire made, not a very big one, and went off to see if it showed. He walked around it in all directions and came back satisfied. He was the most careless fellow of snakes I ever heard of.

"Now get fish," he said, and took his lines and hooks and bait; and off he smashed across the island, leaving Mark and me alone. Maybe you won't believe it, but Mark didn't seem like much company. There was enough of him, goodness knows, but it didn't seem to be the right kind. He told me afterward he felt the same way about me. He sat on top of a stump close to the fire, with his feet pulled up out of danger and a club in his hand. I was on another stump and if my club was smaller than his it wasn't my fault. I got the biggest one I could find.

"Well," says he (it was the first good chance we'd had to talk since I came sprawling into the boat) "where'd you come from all of a s-s-sudden?"

"Batten and Bill found out I wasn't a ghost," says I.

"Purty lucky they did," says he.

"You wouldn't 'a' thought so if they'd been chasin' *you*," I told him; and he wouldn't, neither.

"It was opportunity," he says. "I've heard tell of lots of opportunities, but I never seen one that come in so h-h-handy." It took him half a minute to get out the last word.

"Zadok Biggs said somethin' like that. I met him a piece down the road, or I'd never have got back."

"I wouldn't 'a' come rampin' through that marsh like you did for a farm," says he.

"You'd 'a' sunk in so deep it would 'a' taken two teams of horses to drag you out," says I. "How'd you manage to git the engine out of the house?"

Then he told me all about it like I've told you at the beginning of this chapter, and that was the first I knew about just what had happened.

It wasn't comfortable perching on stumps with our feet hauled up, but we were a lot easier in our minds that way, especially as we kept hearing things fussing around in the grass.

"There goes one rattlin' off there," I says; and I pulled my feet up farther and gripped my club.

"I h-h-hear him," Mark said, kind of strangled-like. I could see him squirming around trying to get more of him up higher on the stump.

We kept hearing rattlers, or thinking we heard them, which was just as bad; and every time one whirred we wished our stumps were full-grown trees and we were sitting on the top branches. The fire was close, but not close enough, and we kept getting hungrier and hungrier. It was good and dark by that time, and the woods looked plenty spooky. Take it altogether, and we weren't having a very good time of it. Even if we did have the engine we weren't what you could call happy about it, and you can't blame us.

Sammy was gone maybe an hour, but when he came back it was worth the waiting, for he had a good bass and six or seven bullheads. The bass was just luck, but the bullheads were easy to get. You can catch them by the dozen all along the river when it gets dark.

Sammy got out his knife, and so did Mark and I. Between us we cleaned those fish in no time and had them sizzling and smelling over the fire. There wasn't a thing to eat with them, only a little salt and pepper; but when we were through there wasn't anything left but bones, and some of *them* were gnawed pretty bad. When a fellow gets so hungry he'll gnaw fishbones he must be pretty close to starvation.

I was beginning to get considerably sleepy, and Mark's head nodded once or twice, but with the snakes around I couldn't quite see my way clear to lying down on the ground. I tried to imagine I could go to sleep sitting on the stump, but I couldn't make myself believe I could do it.

"I'm sleepy," I said to Mark.

"Me, too," says he.

"Goin' to lay down on the ground?"

"Well, I g-g-guess not. I'm goin' to make a snake-proof bed."

"G'wan," says I, for I didn't see how he was going to manage it.

After all, it wasn't so hard. Mark got up courage to come down off his stump, but he didn't wander far away. He cut four saplings with crotches in them and trimmed them into stakes that looked like Y's. He drove these into the soft ground so they stuck up more than a foot in the air, and then fitted long poles for the frames, and made cross-pieces like the slats of a bed. In between he filled with short limbs and leaves and things to make it soft to lie on. When it was all done it was as comfortable a bed as a fellow could want, and safe! Mark climbed on it and lay down.

"Um!" says I. "Guess I'll make me one."

Sammy watched us both all the time, chuckling and grinning and winking and blinking. He didn't go about making any bed, but just gathered more dry wood for the fire and threw himself down on the grass. It wasn't long before he was asleep, and the way he snored would have made a dinner-horn jealous. He'd begin high up and sort of slide way down low. Then he'd start out low and strangle and rumble and snort. Then he'd puff out his cheeks and blow like he was trying to blow out a lamp. He had more than a dozen different kinds of snores. It seemed like he could snore half an hour without repeating the same noise.

"Maybe Sammy don't know much," I says to Mark, "but he's sure a mighty skilful snorer."

CHAPTER XVI

Did you ever try to sleep on a rattlesnake-proof bed on a poison-ivy island? Well, if that was all there was to it it isn't likely you'd drop right off into a doze and have pleasant dreams. But throw in for good measure that two men like Batten and Bill were out looking for you; and if you close your eyes a wink, then I'm pretty much mistaken.

Mark and I tried to sleep. I know I shut my eyes and pretended I was at home with father and mother in the next room. Somehow that didn't do much good—I couldn't pretend hard enough, I guess. Then I tried counting sheep jumping over a fence, but the sheep jumped so slow that I had time in between to figure what Batten would do to us if he caught us. I counted up to a thousand, and watched an imaginary wheel go round and round. But in spite of everything I could think of I was just as wide awake at the end as I was at the beginning.

Mark was perfectly still, and of course I didn't know whether he was asleep or awake. Everything except Sammy was still, too still altogether for comfort. When things are so quiet you just *have* to listen. You can't help it if it was to save your life; and I didn't want to listen. Listening for something you don't hear makes you shivery. I don't know but that it was more scary than the night we sat up by the cave before we knew what Sammy was. I couldn't help imagining a rattler was trying to climb the leg of my bed, and every snap of a twig or rustle of a leaf I turned into a man sneaking through the underbrush.

Besides, there was Sammy snoring for dear life. Just you get into a tight place like we were in and have the only person you can depend on start to snore! I tell you, you feel even lonesomer than if nobody was there at all. I was mad at Sammy, mad all the way through. It didn't seem right that anybody should be comfortable and happy when I was so miserable. Once I made up my mind to yell at Sam, but then I thought how hard he'd been working for us, and kept still.

After a while I couldn't stand it any longer, though, so I raised my head and whispered, cautious, "Oh, Mark, are you awake?"

"Awake!" he says, cross-like. "If I was as sound asleep as I'm w-w-wide awake an earthquake wouldn't rouse me."

"Let's talk," says I; "it'll seem more sociable."

We started in to talk, but there didn't seem to be anything to talk about but snakes and Batten and Bill. The more you talk about things that scare you the more afraid you get, so our conversation wasn't what you'd call a success. We both laid back and kept quiet.

I don't know whether it was two hours or fifteen minutes after that when I sat up straight and listened. I thought I heard voices out on the river, and I sat there stiff, holding my breath, with chills running up and down my spine ten to the minute. For a while I didn't hear another thing; then, up the river some place, something creaked. It isn't natural to hear something creaking out on the water, for fish don't creak, and neither does water. It's surprising how few things there are that *do* creak that aren't made by men. Just listen around and see. As soon as I heard that sound I knew it couldn't be anything else but an oar-lock, and an oar-lock meant a rowboat, and a rowboat meant Batten and Bill. Nobody else would be poking around the river at that time of night.

"Mark," I says, my voice trembling in spite of all I could do to keep it steady.

"Yes," he answered, right off.

"Did you hear it?"

"Yes."

"It must be Batten and Bill."

"L-l-l-lookin' for us!" he sputtered.

"What'll we do?"

"Sammy—wake Sammy."

"Go and wake him," says I, for I didn't like to put my feet down on that ground for fear of stepping right in the middle of a rattler.

We didn't dare call Sammy, for fear of being overheard; and it wasn't safe to throw a stick at him, because he might wake up and holler. There was nothing for it but to take a chance with the snakes.

"Come on," says I. But I didn't trust my feet on the ground till I'd found my club. I took it and reached all around as far as I could, thumping the earth so if there were any rattlers hanging around they'd be scared away, or at least rattle so we'd know where they were. I didn't hear anything, so I made up my mind it would be safe for a little ways at least.

We got down and made for Sammy as quietly as we could go. Sam lay with one arm over his head and the other across his face, and his mouth open wide enough to take in an apple. Mark tickled the palm of his hand, but Sammy only closed his fingers. Then I tapped him on the cheek. Sam just slapped at me like I was a mosquito. It was plain Sammy was a sound sleeper.

There wasn't anything left but to shake him good and hard, so Mark shook. As soon as he did he slapped his hand over Sammy's mouth so he couldn't holler, but that isn't what Sam did at all. He just heaved himself onto his feet all at once and grabbed Mark with his big hands. He'd have broken him in two if I hadn't spoken quick.

"Sammy," says I, as sharp as I could, "it's us—Mark and me."

He came to in a minute and grinned at us sheepish-like.

"Sammy most bust fat boy," he said. "Sammy wake up quick. Scairt. He grab—no find out who."

"Hush," whispers Mark. "There's a boat a-comin' down the river."

"Batten come? Bill come? Eh?"

"I guess so. C-c-couldn't be anybody else."

"Sammy go see." Off went Sammy as quiet as a fish in the water, leaving us all alone.

"Let's stamp out what's left of the fire," says I.

It had burned almost out, but we trampled the coals, and when they were black we covered the place with brush so nobody'd know there had been any fire at all. Now it was as dark as if we were in somebody's pocket, and mighty uncomfortable, I can tell you. Both of us made for our beds and sat on them with our feet pulled up, to wait for Sammy.

In no time he was back. I didn't hear him coming, but all at once he was there. It was just as if he'd popped up out of the ground.

"Who is it?" Mark whispered.

"Batten and Bill," says Sammy.

"Where are they?"

"In boat. Come along island slow, very slow. Look here, look there. Goin' to land, Sammy think."

It was a nice pickle, wasn't it? There were two grown men against a couple of kids and a queer-headed Indian. Of course, Sammy was so big he was a comfort, but, then, there was no telling what Batten and Bill would manage to do.

"Can we hide away from them, Sammy?" I wanted to know, and I wanted to know quick.

"Can't hide if men hunt good. Try, maybe."

"And we can't hide the boat and the turbine," says Mark. "They'd rather have the engine than us."

That was a fact, all right. If the men took to searching the island they'd find my boat hauled up on the shore of the bayou, and they'd get back the turbine. All our work and trouble would be for nothing.

"We got to keep them from l-l-landing," says Mark. He was so excited and anxious I thought he'd never get through stuttering over "landing."

"Sammy throw men in river." He grinned and shook his head and opened and shut his great big hands as though it would be quite a joke to give Batten and Bill a ducking.

But Mark didn't want that; besides, he didn't know if Sammy could manage both the men. What we wanted was to find some scheme that would keep the men from landing at all. I just sat still and waited, because Mark is the schemer of the party. I'm no good that way, and I knew if Mark couldn't think up something there was no use for me to try.

"Sammy," says Mark, "maybe you can do it." He spoke slow, so as not to stutter. "There's a chance of scarin' 'em off."

"Sammy do it. Sure. Sammy yell like panther, eh?"

"No, Sammy won't yell like a panther. Sammy will keep quiet like a f-f-fish till I get through."

Sammy showed his white teeth, and I could almost hear him purr. It tickled him all over every time Mark spoke to him, and it didn't make any difference what he said, either.

"You got to pretend you're a rattlesnake," says Mark. "Go quiet as you can to the shore wherever they try to land. Hide so's they can't see you. Then as soon's one of 'em puts a f-f-foot ashore you rattle. Understand?"

"Sammy know. To be sure. Sammy go kr-r-r-r-r."

I jumped and looked around before I thought. It was the rattlesnakiest noise you ever heard.

"That's it," says Mark. "Now hurry!"

Mark stayed where he was because he couldn't move very quiet. No matter how careful and still he tried to be, he would have sounded like a cow mired in a swamp. There are good things about being fat, but there are bad ones, too, and that was one of the bad ones. I went along with Sammy as far as I dared and then hid behind some bushes. Sammy crawled along to the very edge of the water and kept even with the boat, which had come into sight and was rowing along about twenty feet out. From where I was I could hear Batten and Bill talking to each other low and cautious.

"I'm not crazy to go ashore," says Batten. "That island's alive with snakes."

"Bosh!" says Bill. "Who's afraid of snakes?"

"You come from the city, or you wouldn't be sticking up your nose at rattlers. I bet you never saw a rattler."

"If I did see one I wouldn't run away from it."

"Um!" grunts Batten.

"There's a chance they're hiding there," Bill went on, in a minute. "We went all around it and then down-stream without catching a glimpse of them. I believe they stopped off here and hid."

"We'll soon find out, anyhow," Batten says, and turned the boat toward the shore. "You're not afraid of snakes," he says, sort of sneering, "so you step out first. Don't be afraid."

I couldn't see Sammy, but I could see Batten and Bill. A couple of strokes of the oars brought the boat up against the marshy shore. I could hear the keel grate against the bottom.

"Out you go," says Batten, and Bill stood up and stepped ashore.

Then Sammy rattled. "Kr-r-r-r-r-r," he went. It sounded as if it was right under Bill's feet. Well, sir, you should have seen Bill jump. He didn't even wait to turn around, but just went up in the air backward and let out a yell as loud as a locomotive whistle. He landed one foot in the boat and the other in the water.

"No," says Batten, and I bet he was grinning mean, "*you* wouldn't run away from a snake, you wouldn't. Oh no!"

"I most stepped on him," Bill says, shaky-like. "When he struck he just missed my leg. I felt him." Now, that shows you what a fellow's imagination will do for him, especially if he's startled.

"Try again," Batten says. "He's probably gone by now."

"Try yourself if you want to. If you expect me to step on this confounded island you row to some other spot."

They argued about it a while and then pushed off. When they started away Sammy followed after, and I went along, too. I was so interested I plumb forgot about snakes myself. They rowed about a hundred feet and then tried it again, but Sammy was there first. As soon as Bill put his foot on the ground away went that Kr-r-r-r-r-r, and back he scrambled into the boat.

"Must be alive with them," he panted. "Hear that one?"

HE LET OUT A YELL AS LOUD AS A LOCOMOTIVE WHISTLE

"I heard him," says Batten. "We'll try another place."

They tried again three times, but every time Sammy was there to rattle. At the last place Bill got mad at Batten and says: "This is a fool thing, prowling around this island. Nobody ever landed on it—there's a snake under every blade of grass.

If you want to go ashore, all right; but me, I'll stay right in the boat, engine or no engine."

"They do seem sort of thick," Batten says; and he didn't make any offer to go ashore himself. "We might as well go home. Tomorrow we can set out to look for them again." He stopped a minute and says, "Changed your opinion of rattle-snakes, Bill?"

Bill just grunted, and then they rowed off up the river and out of our sight.

We were pretty relieved, I tell you. After that we were sure the men wouldn't bother us any more that night, so we went to bed again. It wasn't long before I fell asleep, and I guess the others did, too. Anyhow, I didn't know another thing till Sammy shook me next morning. It wasn't light yet, but Mark was up and ready.

"They said they'd be lookin' for us this m-m-mornin'," he said, "so we better be stirrin'. It's half past three now."

The first thing to do was to haul out the boat and see how badly smashed it was, and to do that we had to take the turbine out on shore. Mark and I got big clubs and stood right by Sammy while Sammy worked. He killed one rattler with eight rattles on his tail the first thing, and between us we got three more before Sammy had the boat up and turned over. One plank was split and sprung out so that there was a big gap for the water to run through. It wasn't nearly as bad as it might have been, and Sammy wasn't any time fixing it up with the little ax. It wasn't as good as new, by any means, but the water couldn't leak in very fast. Mark figured he and I could bail while Sammy rowed, and so keep the thing afloat.

Mark was too anxious to get home with the turbine to bother about breakfast, so we started off, rowing and bailing, and didn't have any trouble to speak of. It was a fine bright morning, with the sun coming down so clean and shiny and light that it looked as if it was something being poured all over everything—something you could touch. I've seen lots of spring mornings like that, when the sunlight didn't seem like sunlight at all, but as if it were a kind of dew that made every leaf and stone and the water, and even animals and folks, sort of glow. Mark was a great fellow for noticing things like that, even when he had worries on his mind, and he kept talking about it all the way down the river.

Along toward the last the boat commenced to leak pretty bad again. I guess it was the weight of the turbine pressing down on the weak board, so Mark decided to stop at the cave and hide the engine there while somebody went into town for a wagon to haul it in. It was a pretty hard pull getting it up on the hill and into the cave, but we managed it, and Mark and I were able to help with a rope that we had there. He and I went first with the rope and held the engine from slipping back when Sammy had to put it down to rest. We were pretty tired when the turbine was safe inside the cave, so we lay down and took a little rest.

"Sammy," says Mark, "you stay here and guard the turbine while Tallow and I go to town for help. Don't let anybody git it away from you."

"Sammy watch. Nobody get machine." He got a big club and whirled it around his head so it whistled. "Nobody take it away from Sammy, eh? Sammy guess not."

Mark guessed not, too. He and Sammy and I walked to the road together, and Mark and I were just for starting off toward town when we saw a couple of men coming in a buggy. At first I thought it was Batten and Bill, but it wasn't, and my heart went back where it belonged. We turned to Sammy to say good-by, but a more frightened fellow there never was. His eyes bulged, and his knees sagged, and he was muttering and shaking his head and pointing.

"After Sammy," he chattered. "Take him back to poor-farm. Make Sammy dig in fields. Make him sleep in house." Then all of a sudden the idea of running popped into his head, and without so much as an "Aye," "Yes," or "No" to Mark he turned and scooted down the hill and out of sight.

Sure enough, when we took a good look at the men one of them was Mr. Grey, superintendent of the poor-farm; but it turned out they weren't looking for anybody, but just driving home from the next town, where Mr. Grey had been on business.

That wasn't any help to us, though, for it left us without Sammy just the same, and Sammy seemed to be pretty necessary. We felt we could leave the engine with him and it would be safe. He could guard the mouth of the cave sort of like Horatius at the bridge, and Batten and Bill would find it was close to impossible to chase him off. Now it looked as if either Mark or I would have to go to town, and that would leave just one boy on guard.

"It ain't safe," says I. "Sammy could have done it, but neither of us can alone. I wouldn't even want to try it with both of us here."

"Neither would I," Mark answered. "But what are we going to do?"

"We might send word in by Mr. Grey," I says. "He could send out help."

The buggy was almost to us now, and without thinking how he might frighten the horse Mark stepped into the road and held up his hand. The horse snorted, jerked back, and then took the bit in his teeth and tore off as tight as he could go. Mark had to jump quicker than I ever saw him jump before to get out of the way.

It did seem as if luck was against us. We stood there a minute and looked after the rig, which was getting farther away every second.

"Let's get back to the cave and see what there is to do," I says.

Mark never said a word, but just started off with a discouraged hunch to his shoulders, and I trailed after. We sat down in front of the cave, tired, hungry, and pretty sick of the whole business.

CHAPTER XVII

It was early in the morning yet—before seven. Folks in Wicksville were just getting up, but it seemed to Mark and me that we'd been awake a week. For a while we didn't do anything but sit on the sand in front of the cave and wish we had something to eat or that somebody we could trust would come along. But there wasn't a bit of use wishing.

"We should have had a telephone put in the cave," I told Mark. "It certainly would come in handy this morning."

Mark didn't say anything. He just got up and went inside the cave, where he began rummaging around in the hope of finding a few potatoes we had overlooked. There were pans to cook with and fishing-tackle and Ku Klux Klan disguises, but it was precious little good any of them did. I saw him pick up a sheet and hood and stand looking at it.

"Not goin' to try eatin' that, are you?" I called to him.

"No," says he. "I was just wonderin' if we couldn't put the Klan to some good use."

"If we could only signal to Plunk an' Binney."

"But we can't," he says. "What I wish is that I could get my jack-knife to Uncle Ike Bond. He'd know it was a signal to hurry to the cave, and he *would* hurry."

"That's right," says I. "We never used any signs on him just for fun. He warned us about that. If we could get the knife to him he'd know it was serious. But what's the use talkin' about it; we might as well hope for an airship to come swoopin' down and carry us safely home."

Mark covered up the turbine with sheets and came out where I was. "Let's walk to the road again. No, I'll go to the road, and you stay with the turbine. If anybody comes you holler like s-s-sixty."

"All right," says I; "but don't be gone long."

He climbed up to the road and sat down on a big stone under a butternut tree.

Maybe fifteen minutes went along before he heard anything, and then it was a whistle from up the river way, and the tune it whistled was "Marching Through Georgia."

Then the tin-peddler's red wagon came into sight, with Zadok Biggs sitting on the seat, his head back, as we had first seen him, taking it easy, enjoying the morning, and whistling so the birds must have been jealous. Maybe they thought Zadok

Biggs was some sort of a bird himself; if they did, birds must be able to stretch their imaginations considerable.

Mark never was so glad to see anybody in his life. He stepped out into the road and waited. Zadok came driving along without seeing him until Mark spoke; then he straightened up, looked at Mark, and slapped his leg. He slapped it again and chuckled, and began talking to the horse.

"Rosinante," he says, "there he stands! There stands Marcus Aurelius Fortunatus Tidd. Observe him — look at him is the way people usually say it. Mind what I said about opportunity, Rosinante. Here stands Marcus Aurelius, who has had an opportunity. We shall pause — stop — shall we not, to inquire what he did with it." He swung his little legs sideways over the edge of the seat and stared down at Mark.

"Opportunity," says he, "and Marcus Aurelius Fortunatus. Um! It knocked, so to speak. Were you in?"

"Well," says Mark, "I wasn't f-f-far off."

"Good! Excellent! I said so. I told young Martin you would not disappoint me. I would have been disappointed. I, Zadok Biggs, am your friend, your friend for life, and I would have been grieved. You got the — the turbine?" He shot the last question at Mark like it was a pea out of a pea-blower. It came out with a sort of *poof*.

Mark nodded. "I got it; but it ain't safe yet."

"So? You are perturbed — worried is the commoner word. *I* am not. I have confidence in you. How could one named Marcus Aurelius Fortunatus Tidd let failure roost in the nest of success? A figure of speech that, a sort of metaphor. You understand me?"

"I guess so. What I want to know is, will you do me a f-f-favor?"

"A favor? Will Zadok Biggs do a favor for Marcus Aurelius! Anything, even to the half of my kingdom, as the kings in the Bible used to say. I am yours. Command me!"

"It ain't much. Just take this jack-knife to Uncle Ike Bond, the bus driver. Give it to him and say it's from me."

"Why," says Zadok, surprised, "what's this." He was disappointed, likely, at the littleness and commonness of the favor Mark asked. Then his long, lean face lightened up and he slapped his leg again. "I perceive — understand is the word in general use. It is a token, a signal. Excellent! You are coming up to my expectations. Now who would have expected this?" He leaned over so far Mark thought he'd fall off the wagon, and stared at him so admiringly that Mark blushed. "A remarkable lad," Zadok went on. "My friend for life. Will I deliver the knife? Will I? Will Zadok Biggs? Just pass it up to me and see."

Mark handed up the knife, and Zadok shoved it into his pocket. Then he shook the lines and waked up his horse, who had taken the opportunity to go to sleep, and started off. "I will hasten — hurry is the less dignified word. Uncle Ike Bond shall have the knife. I shall say it comes from Marcus Aurelius, who knows an opportunity when he sees it. Good-by. Remember Zadok Biggs. He is your friend for life. Remember him."

We both felt a little easier in our minds with the message sent to Uncle Ike. Of course we couldn't tell how long he might be coming to us, for sometimes he had to drive folks into the country, and sometimes he was off fishing, so it was possible Zadok Biggs would have considerable bother finding him. But we knew he'd come sometime, and that was better than not having any hope at all.

"Well," says Mark, "we might as well do somethin' while we're waitin'."

"Sure!" says I. "Let's git up a game to pass away the time."

Mark thought a minute. He was fine at getting up new games, because he had read so many histories and books of adventure. All he had to do was to remember some bully story, and right off he'd make a game out of it. "Let's pertend," says he, "that you and me are sentinels left to g-g-guard this treasure-cave. It's got a jewel into it as big as your fist. We'll make b'lieve the turbine is the jewel, and it is worth more'n a billion dollars. There was a party of us captured this jewel out of a heathen temple, and everybody but us had gone to git help. We're bein' pursued by the heathens, and they've found us here, and right this minute they're besiegin' us. How's that?"

"Fine," says I. "I kin see more'n fifty of 'em a-sneakin' around down among the trees and rocks. Looks to me like they was gittin' ready to make a charge."

"We got to git am-am-munition. If our supply gives out we'd be easy prey for em."

So we went to work gathering sling-shot pebbles—nice smooth, round ones. We had to sally out into the open to get them, and that was taking a chance, with all those heathens shooting away at us with bows and arrows; but by ducking and dodging we made out to fill our pockets and get back safe. Between us we had a couple of pecks of stones.

"There," says Mark; "that'll stand 'em off a while."

We got out our sling-shots just in time. The enemy was creeping up on us, thinking to take us by surprise, but we whanged away at them like sharp-shooters, and it was pretty seldom we missed. Mostly we struck the heathen in vital spots, so that they threw up their arms with a screech and fell dead, rolling over down the hill. Twice we stopped regular charges, and in fifteen minutes or so the foe was pretty badly discouraged.

They retreated right down to the shore of the river, where their war-canoes were, with us a-firing after them as fast as we could shoot. Then for the first time we dared take a breath and look around us. It was lucky we did, for there, not a hundred yards off, were Henry C. Batten and Bill landing out of a boat. Batten looked up at us and grinned.

My stomach all of a sudden went hollow, and my knees got so weak I sat down without intending to. Yes, sir, I went right down ker-plunk. Those men popping up like that took the wind clean out of my sails, and no mistake. Mark wasn't any better off, either. He looked like somebody had up and poured a pitcher of ice-water down his back.

If I'd been all alone I'd have up and run, but with Mark there I was ashamed to. He couldn't run, for two reasons: first, he was too fat to go very fast; and, second, he wasn't the running kind. We knew there was help coming, too, but how long it would be before it got here we hadn't the faintest idea; it might come too late.

Mark was scared at first, I could see it, but in a minute he got mad, real good and snapping mad, to think of all the trouble we'd had getting the engine back, and then to have these men drop in when it was most safe. It didn't look fair any way you took it.

"Tallow," says he, "you can do what you want to, but I'm going to stay and *f-f-fight*."

Well, what could I do? I just took a long breath and says, "All right, Mark, but I don't see what good it's goin' to do."

"They sha'n't get that turbine as long as I kin s-s-stand up," he stuttered.

"It looks," says I, "as if we was in for a hard fall, then."

Batten said something to Bill, and both of them started up the bank.

"Git back there," Mark yells.

Batten laughed out loud, which wasn't a very good thing to do. Never laugh at folks when you've got them cornered, because it's likely to get their dander up, and no telling what'll happen. It made me so mad to hear Batten laugh that way that, unconscious-like, I just hauled off with my sling-shot and sailed a pebble down at him. It struck right under his feet, and he jumped like he'd been bitten.

"Hey," he yelled, "quit that, you young grampus!"

"Fine," says Mark, "that's the ticket," and he put a stone in his sling and pelted it so it went whizzing past Batten's ear. Batten stood right still, and so did Bill.

"You keep away from here," yelled Mark, "or I'll shoot straighter. G-g-git!"

"If you hit me with that thing!" calls Batten, threatening-like.

"Come on," says Bill; "they can't hit us. Come on."

They started up again, but they didn't go far, for Mark whanged another pebble at them—and didn't miss. It hit Batten just above the knee, and I bet it stung like sixty. He let a holler out of him and ducked behind a tree. Bill started edging around, but I stopped him with another pebble that whizzed past his head.

Batten was good and mad now, and so was Bill. They kept yelling back and forth at each other, but stayed all the time behind the trees where we couldn't hit them. That satisfied us; we weren't out to shoot anybody with our sling-shots, and didn't want to if they'd only quit pestering us.

"Young feller," Batten yelled up to Mark, "put that thing down or you'll be sorry. Don't you go shootin' it at me again."

"I ain't goin' to shoot so long's you s-s-stay behind that tree," says Mark, "but if you start up here again I'll p-p-paste you, and it won't be in the leg, either."

Bill took the chance to run across an open space to another tree, and got there just in time. The pebble flicked off a chunk of the bark as he got sheltered.

"They're tryin' to divide," says Mark "so's to take us on two sides. Don't let one of 'em get onto the hill above us."

That would make it pretty bad, for it's hard to shoot up-hill; and, besides, a man higher than we were could make it mighty hot for us by rolling things down.

"We'll stop Bill from comin' any higher," I says.

The best way to do that, I thought, was to give him something to think about besides climbing hills, so I looked careful down at the tree he was behind. The only part of him that stuck out was his hand, and that was gripping a sapling close to his tree to hold him from slipping, I expect, for the slope was pretty steep right there.

"Watch me whang his fingers," I says, but, honest, I didn't have much hope of hitting them. I guess it was more good luck than good judgment; but, all the same, I took careful aim, and let her fly. The stone whizzed down and banged Bill's thumb a good one so he yelped out sharp and danced into the open, shaking his hand like he wanted to flop it off. He wasn't exactly quiet about saying things to us, either. If he'd done to Mark and me what he said he was going to do we couldn't have been worth carrying home.

"Always f-f-follow up your victories," says Mark, with a grin. "I'll give him another while he's feeling bad." This one took him a clip right on the hip where his pants were tight, and Bill didn't wait around there any longer. Out where he stood was a bad place, he thought, so he turned tail and made for the trees lower on the hill.

"That's right," yells Mark; "you'll like it better down there."

We could see Batten edging over toward Bill. He was too far off for us to take a crack at him, but he went careful, just the same, with one eye on us all the time. It was pretty evident neither of them liked our sling-shots very much, and I don't blame them. A pebble the size of a good marble stings when it's snapped by a couple of strong rubbers. You can shoot hard enough to kill a squirrel or rabbit, and, while it wouldn't damage a man very much, it would hurt like fury. I've figured it out that soldiers in a battle aren't so much afraid of being killed or badly injured as they are of being hurt. It's the idea of *pain* that scares them, and we could give Batten and Bill about all the pain they wanted.

"There's only one way they can get us," says Mark, "and that's to charge."

"Yes," says I, "if they got the grit to keep a-comin', no matter how hard we hit 'em, we're beat."

Batten and Bill had their heads together way down by the river. Every once in a while they'd turn and look or point up to us, so we knew they were hatching up a plan of attack. After a while they stood and studied out the lay of the land.

The cave was about two-thirds up the hill. Mostly the climb was pretty steep, and there were lots of big rocks and boulders and trees until you got maybe a hundred feet from the cave, and there was an open space steeper than the rest. The cave faced on a sort of shelf that stuck out maybe ten feet from the door. Probably it was made by the earth that was dug out of the cave when it was made. Partly that, anyhow, and partly made by cutting the face of the hill smooth and straight. When you make a snow house you generally start by heaping up snow and tamping it down till it's about the shape of a half-orange. Then when you start to hollow out and make your door, you cut away one side so it's straight up and down—just slice it off to give you a place to begin. That's what the folks who dug the cave had done—cut out a chunk of the hill like a big step, L-shaped, and the foot of the L was the little shelf in front of our door.

The hill went up perpendicular about six feet from the top of the door and then slanted away natural again, getting less steep as it came nearer the level ground above.

That, in a general way, is how the land lay.

Batten and Bill studied it over quite a while and then got their heads together again. They seemed to be arguing about something. Batten smashed one hand against the other impatient-like, and it looked as though he was ordering Bill to do what he wanted. We waited to see what that would be.

Both the men started up the hill, but they didn't get out from behind things any more than they had to. From one tree to another and from one boulder to the next they went slinking until they were almost at the edge of the clear space in front of the cave.

"They're going to charge," says Mark. "Get ready."

I filled my pocket with pebbles and stood, all trembly, waiting for them to begin.

All of a sudden they both let out yells and started scrambling up toward us as fast as they could. That wasn't very fast, on account of the steepness and loose sand and stones that kept slipping back, but they came like they had made up their minds to get us in spite of everything.

Just the minute they got uncovered we began to shoot. I was surprised to see how little scared I really was when things began to happen; and Mark, why, he was as cool as a cucumber, and took careful aim every time before he let fly.

We shot pretty well, too. Of course, we didn't hit every time, but we hit often enough, and the closer they came the oftener we hit. They didn't say a word, and Mark and I were too busy to speak.

They got over the first twenty-five feet all right, and started in on the next twenty-five. Now they were near enough so that any fellow who could shoot at all would have hard work to miss. And we shot fast. Plunk! plunk! plunk! we would hear the stones as they struck. They kept on, though, for another fifteen or twenty feet until they were only about fifty feet away and maybe forty feet lower than we were. That gave us all the advantage, of course, for it's hard enough to climb a steep hill without having a couple of fellows peppering at you from the top.

"I'll shoot faster than you can talk," says I, making a little fun of his stuttering.

We did shoot fast and hard. Every time I pulled back the rubber as far as it would stretch, and I bet those pebbles hurt some. They hurt more than Batten and Bill could stand, anyhow, for in another minute they had enough. First Bill quit and went leaping down the hill; then Batten, finding out he was all alone, gave up and retreated so fast Mark said it was a rout.

We didn't let them go without hurrying them along, either. Just as long as they were in sight we kept on whanging at them, and I'll make a guess that there weren't two men in the state who had more black-and-blue spots to show than they did when they got to the bottom. We laughed so loud they could hear us when we saw them rubbing their sore places.

Batten shook his fist at us, and Bill roared something we couldn't understand.

All the while they were talking together and motioning. Then they turned like they were giving it up and got into their boat.

"Whoop!" I yelled, "we've licked 'em!"

Mark shook his head. "No," he says. "It's a—a—s-s-s-stratagem."

"A what?" says I.

"A s-s-s-s-s—" Mark started in, hissing like the exhaust of an engine.

"Better try some other word," I told him; and he grinned as good-natured as could be.

"It's a trick," he says.

"That's better. Leave the s's alone when you're excited."

"They're trying to make us think they've quit so they can s-s-s—"

"There you go."

"Sneak up on us," he finished.

Batten and Bill pushed their boat off and rowed down-stream. We watched them till they went out of sight around the bend.

"I bet they're gone," I said.

Mark only shook his head.

"I'm goin' to see," says I.

"Go ahead, but don't let 'em catch you. Don't go blunderin' along. Be c-careful."

"I'll be careful," says I; and with that I started off along the face of the hill in the direction Batten and Bill had taken.

CHAPTER XVIII

I scrambled along, edging up toward the top of the bank, and when I got there I started to run along on the level ground. I couldn't run very fast on account of the underbrush and because every little ways the rain had washed out gullies that I had to go around or jump over. I followed the shore of the river, keeping my eyes peeled all the time for a sight of Batten and Bill. There were so many trees between me and the water that I couldn't see far; but I could watch the shore-line, as I went along, to discover if they had landed. After I got around the bend I went more carefully, for I wasn't a bit anxious to have them know I was spying on them. I kept behind the clumps of sumach and suchlike shrubs that grew all along the hillside, wherever it was possible; and when it wasn't I went back a few yards from the top of the slope, where I couldn't be seen by anybody standing at the water's edge.

It seemed I must have caught up with the boat if they hadn't rowed faster than a horse can gallop, so I crept up back of a clump of bushes and looked down. I couldn't see a thing. Nobody was in sight, and the woods were as still and calm-like as could be. There are places along the shore that look as if folks had never been there, and this was one of them. Cat-tails and reeds grew out into the river from the bank, and hazel and sumach and elderberry bushes filled in thick between the big trees. It wasn't a swampy place exactly, though it was pretty soft and squashy in the spring when the water was high, but it *looked* marshy.

Where the boat had gone I couldn't figure out, for from where I was now I could see a quarter of a mile down the river and quite a ways up and down the shore. The only live thing anywhere around was a red-headed woodpecker that propped himself up against the side of a butternut tree and pecked away like he was paid to do it by the hour.

"Huh," says I to myself, "that's funny." I sat there scratching my head awhile, and then made up my mind to slide down the back to explore closer. It was steep there, almost dead up and down, but there were bushes and things to hang on to, so I didn't think anything about it at all, but just turned around and started down crab-fashion, feet first and with my face toward the ground. Probably I was a quarter of the way down when I stepped on a loose bit of earth which went slipping out from under me. I grabbed out at a wild-rose bush, prickers and all, but missed, and went pell-mell, head over heels, down to the bottom, tearing chunks out of my clothes and scuffing off patches of skin.

When I landed *bump* at the bottom I lay still a minute to find out if I was busted any place; but there wasn't anything wrong outside of scratches and bruises, so I sat up and looked to see just where I'd fetched up. I saw all right. Not more than six feet away from me were Batten and Bill a-grinning at me like a pair of Cheshire cats.

"Good morning," says Batten, polite-like. "You come down a little sudden, didn't you?"

I was so startled and mad I didn't answer a word. I'd made a pretty mess of things for sure, coming tumbling right down into Batten's arms that way. All they would have to do was just step up and grab me. That would mean that Mark would be left all alone to guard the cave, and it wouldn't be any job at all for Batten and Bill to get him. They would just have to divide and come at him from different ways. If one man came uphill from below and another came down at the cave from above, what chance would Mark have? Not a bit.

I couldn't even give him warning, for it was too far to holler. I felt pretty mean, I can tell you. I was a nice kind of a scout to send out, wasn't I? To go sprawling right into the enemy's hands the first thing!

Bill was laughing so he had to lean up against a tree, and Batten was standing about six feet off and grinning as mean as could be. It was evident they thought they had me safe, and I thought so, too; but nobody ever did anything without trying first. I couldn't be any worse off if I tried to get away, and I might make a go of it if I was quick. I didn't think about it more than a second, but rolled over and over a couple of times, leaped to my feet, and went a-kiting upstream toward the cave.

Batten let out a surprised yell and came jumping after me, with Bill right behind him, sort of barking at every step he took. I had started off so quick, and it took them so all of a sudden, that I got a lead of most twenty feet, which wasn't enough by any manner of means. Two hundred would have suited me better.

I couldn't climb the hill, the river headed me off on the other side, and so there was only one way for me to go, and that was right along the edge of the water. It was the best way, anyhow, because it was clearer of underbrush and shrubs. I stood a chance of beating them in a clear space, but they could push their way through bushes faster than I because they were stronger. I put my head down and ran.

Back of me I heard Batten and Bill floundering and plunging. They didn't yell after the start—saving their breath, I guess—but just kept after me as fast as they could come. I didn't know whether they were gaining or not; and I didn't dare turn my head to see, for fear of tripping over something. It was pretty certain I couldn't get to Mark, for that would mean climbing the hill, but I might tire the men out by running on straight ahead. Anyhow, if they didn't catch me too soon I could get close enough to the cave to yell and warn Mark, and that was the chief thing to think about. "He mustn't be taken by surprise! He mustn't be taken by surprise!" I kept saying to myself over and over again.

Another hundred feet, and I would be around the bend of the river, where my voice would carry to the cave; and I made up my mind I'd get that far if I had to blow up and bust for it. I was getting tired, and my lungs hurt, and my heart was going as if it said, "Choke, choke, choke," but I let out another notch and went faster than before. It was just a final spurt. A fellow always has that left in him, that last spurt. I never could understand it; no matter how fast you're going, it seems as if you could go a little bit faster just at the last if it is necessary.

I was around the point now, and, sitting in front of the cave, I could see Mark Tidd, looking like a big fat statue. He was as still as if he had been a stone.

"Mark!" I screeched. "Look out, Mark! They're after me!"

The next thing I heard was somebody smashing and sprawling onto the ground behind me. Either Batten or Bill had tripped—I don't know which. That left only one man chasing me, and, somehow, it made my breath come freer and my legs work easier. Maybe it was what I've heard folks call "second wind." At any rate, I kept on and on, until pretty soon the noise behind me got farther away and at last stopped. But *I* didn't stop. Not a bit of it. There would be no stopping for me until I'd got a lot more distance between me and those men than there was now.

As soon as I thought I was safe I turned off to the left and scrambled up the hill. You can believe I was careful now. I crawled almost every foot of the way when I started circling back to Mark, but I got there at last. It seemed like a long time; but most likely it wasn't more than fifteen or twenty minutes after Batten and Bill quit chasing me when I peeked over the brow of the hill down onto the cave. I lay there quiet, not making a sound, because it came into my head I might be more useful as a surprise party than if I went right down to reinforce Mark. So I scrambled around and filled my pockets with pebbles, to be ready when I was needed.

Batten and Bill sat down by the edge of the river getting back their breath. As soon as they were rested again they got onto their feet and started up-hill like they meant business. Mark stood up and took his sling-shot in his hand; and I tell you I was proud of him, the way he made ready to fight all alone without a soul he knew of to help him.

Before they came to the clearing the men separated. Batten came straight up, but Bill forked off to the right to do what Mark called "execute a flank movement." He was going to come at the cave from the side while Batten charged from the front. It was a pretty desperate situation. Mark couldn't shoot in two directions at once, and while he was peppering one man the other could sneak up and grab him from the back. I guess he figured he was licked, but that didn't stop him from fighting to the last second. He was gritty, and no mistake.

"Hum," says I to myself, "I'll just give you a surprise party, Mister Bill." So I slid down in the thick of a mess of hazel bushes, and from them behind a big boulder, always keeping where neither Batten nor Bill could see me, until I was almost over the cave. Then I sat back and grinned.

Bill kept wallowing up the slope, while Batten waited just below the clearing, out of range. When Bill was in position Batten yelled, and both of them dashed for the cave. Mark didn't pay any attention to Bill. He figured it out, I guess, that the fight was about over, anyhow, and he'd devote all his time to making Batten sorry he came. And he did, too! The way he peppered that man 'most made me laugh out loud. But Batten kept on coming because he knew Bill was on the way.

Well, in about two minutes Bill came out where I could get a whack at him. I put a nice big pebble in my sling and aimed at his hat. *Spat* went the pebble, and off flew the hat, and Bill brought up sudden. He couldn't see me, and kept looking all around to find out where the stone came from. The second he turned his head I let him have it again hard. He yelped.

Then I spoke soft to Mark. "Go for Batten," says I. "I'm right here, and I'll look after Bill." I heard him chuckle.

"What's the matter?" Batten yelled, savage.

"The other kid's there somewheres shootin' me," says Bill.

"Keep on after him," Batten says.

Bill started, but I stung him again, and he stopped. "Not me," he says, and began edging away. Batten saw it wasn't any use, so he turned and got out, too.

Then I slid down to the cave.

"They most got me!" says I.

"It l-l-looked that way when you was goin' past," says Mark. "My, but you can run!" His little eyes were twinkling away, and his lips were working like he wanted to laugh.

"Go ahead! Laugh!" I told him. "Where'd you be if I hadn't showed up?"

Sammy's little ax was lying out in front of the cave, and there was a pile of shavings by the door.

"What you been doing?" I asked him.

"Oh, just cutting out these things," says he, and pointed to three or four pieces of sapling trunk about twice as long and thick as towel-rollers, over on the sand.

"Cuttin' stove-wood?"

"Nope. Just thought they might come in handy," says he.

I didn't ask any more about them, because I saw right off he had some kind of a scheme; and when Mark has a scheme the only thing to do is wait till he gets ready to tell you about it. You could ask him questions all day, and never get a hint of what he was up to.

I went into the cave and looked around, casual-like. There was the engine. I couldn't see it, really, because it was all covered up by the sheets; but I could tell it was there, and I felt pretty proud to think we'd been able to get it back. The thing now was to keep it, and so far we'd done average well.

I came out with a pail in my hand. "I'm thirsty," says I. "I wonder if there ain't some way to get a drink?"

"Wish there was," says Mark, "but I don't see how."

"Maybe I could get up over the hill and around to the spring."

"Better not try; you had enough bad luck last time you went away."

Well, that made me kind of mad, so I started up the bank.

"Wait!" Mark called. "Lemme go! I'm all cramped up sittin' here."

I came back and gave him the pail, but just then we saw Batten and Bill moving around among the trees, so we gave up the idea of getting water and went on watch again. Mark stayed on the shelf in front of the cave, and I went back up above again where I hid when I took Bill by surprise.

I settled down, with my back against a stone as big as a bushel-basket, and made myself as comfortable as I could. The stone was right over the cave entrance, just sort of stuck into the dirt which held it where it was. It interested me, and I got up to examine it close—it would be the easiest thing in the world to pry it loose and send it bumping down the hill. I was going to do it just for fun; then an idea hit me. I would save up that stone right where it was. It looked to me like it could be made to come in pretty handy.

It wasn't any good mentioning it to Mark, but I went down and borrowed Sammy's little ax, which I used to cut down a tree as big around as my wrist. I trimmed all the limbs off it and laid it down alongside of the stone. Then I sat down and took it easy.

The sun was shining bright and warm; the sand was soft and comfortable to lie on; and a fine breeze was blowing that made you want to close your eyes and doze. It must have been close to eleven o'clock now, which meant we'd been up a long time. We'd been considerably busy since we got up, too, and I was tired and sore all over; so I says to myself I'd shut my eyes just a minute, but wouldn't go to sleep. That was all right to say, but—well, the next thing I remember was Mark hollering at me loud as he could yell.

I sat up quick, just in time to see Batten dodge out from behind some bushes not more than thirty feet from the cave and come clawing toward Mark. I didn't see Bill anywhere just then, but I had sense enough to turn around and look up the hill. There was Bill plunging down toward me.

For a minute it looked as though the jig was up, as Uncle Ike Bond says, but then I thought of that big stone and the lever I'd made to pry it with. I jumped for it, and dug it into the dirt. "Mark," I yelled, "duck into the cave! Quick!"

I heard him scramble, and knew he was doing what I said. He wasn't the kind to stop and ask questions in an emergency. When I yelled he knew I had a good reason, so he just did what I said.

Batten was right in line with the cave now where the stone would come smashing down on him, and the place was so steep he couldn't get out of the way quick enough to dodge. I had him right where I wanted him, so I stood up and yelled.

He saw me, with the lever back of the stone, and let out a frightened squeak. His face got as white as a goose's back, and he hung there to a shrub, too scared to move.

Bill was coming down at me, but he was too far away to do any good. I turned around to him and called: "Mister Bill, you stop right where you are. If you come another step I'll heave this boulder down onto Batten and squash him. Don't come another step."

Bill stopped and looked, and when he saw just how things were he turned kind of green.

"Go on back!" I says. "Git a move on!"

He didn't say a word, but just wheeled around and did as I told him.

"Now," I says to Batten, "you git, too. I won't heave it if you mosey along."

He didn't stop to argue, but rolled over and half slid, half fell down the hill. I never would have pushed over that stone. I couldn't have done it; but, then, Batten and Bill didn't know.

So far the siege had been going our way, but nobody had come to relieve us, and we didn't know when they would. I'd have given my new jack-knife to have heard Uncle Ike Bond hollering back in the road.

CHAPTER XIX

"They won't try *that* again," I said.

"No; 'tain't likely. But they'll try somethin'. Don't you ever b'lieve they're goin' to g-g-give up."

"We've got 'em beat easy," says I.

Mark shook his head. "I could tell 'em somethin'," says he, "that would lick us in a minute."

"It's lucky we're fightin' against them instead of you," says I, sarcastic-like. "How'd you go about it to capture the cave?"

"Well," says he, "the first thing I'd do would be to make sh-sh-sh-sh—"

"Whistle," says I.

"Shields," he finished up with a rush.

Nothing to it, was there, except thinking of it? It would be the simplest thing in the world for Batten and Bill to come climbing right up in our faces if they were sheltered from our pebbles behind some kind of a shield. They could keep right on a-coming and laugh at us while they were doing it.

"They'll never think of it," says I.

"It's only a question of time," stuttered Mark. "What I'm wonderin' is, will they think of it before help comes from Wicksville?"

It looked as if Batten and Bill were going to settle down to starve us out—a regular siege. They knew, of course, that we two boys couldn't carry off the engine; but, then, they must have guessed that they couldn't keep us bottled up very long. They had seen Sammy, and Sammy was gone. If I had been in their shoes I would have reasoned out that he was gone for help. We knew he wasn't gone for anything but to get away from the poor-farm man, but what we knew didn't help Batten and Bill.

We sat and watched them, and they sat and watched us. Once in a while one of them would get up and move around, but for a half-hour by Mark's watch they didn't make a hostile advance.

"They ain't got as much sense as I give 'em credit for," Mark says.

"I hope they don't git more'n they've got," says I.

"If they hain't clean foolish," he says, "they'll figger it out pretty soon."

"If it was back in the time of knights and armor and them things," I told him, "they'd think of shields quick. But nobody civilized has used sich things for hundreds of years. Men jest stand up and git shot. That's why they don't git the idee. Maybe Batten and Bill ain't educated so's they know about armor."

"I should think," says Mark, deliberate-like, "they'd *git* educated. Nobody'd have to shoot me with pebbles more'n a dozen times before I thought of gittin' behind somethin' or other."

Men are never as quick planning things as boys. And when they do scheme something out it generally isn't as good. You take a boy and he'll hit on more good things in an hour than a man will in a week. It doesn't look to me as though imaginations grew up with most men; they leave them behind somewheres before they git old enough to vote.

After a while we saw Bill jump up and take a jack-knife out of his pocket. He looked around searching, and then went over to a clump of willows which he began to cut down and throw in a pile.

"What's that for?" I wanted to know.

Mark scratched his head. "They've decided on somethin'," says he, "but what it is I don't see clear."

Bill kept on cutting and cutting till he had a big pile of green boughs. When he had enough he sat down by them with his back toward us and began doing something to them—we couldn't see what.

"He's makin' some sort of a contraption," I says.

"I'll bet," says Mark, "it's some kind of a sh-sh-sh—"

"Shield," I finished for him.

"That's it," says he.

Batten walked over by Bill and commenced to work, too. They fiddled around ten or fifteen minutes, and we could hear them talking and laughing, but they were so far away we couldn't hear what they said. I wished we could have.

Mark drew a long breath. "This," says he, "is the end of the battle. We're licked!"

"Maybe not."

He just smiled sort of regretful. "We're licked," he says again, "but we hain't disgraced. We kept on fightin' as long as we could."

"And we'll keep on some more," I said sharp. "They ain't got us or the turbine yet."

"They'll git us," he says, and then grinned sly-like, with that cunning look to his eyes that always comes into them when he's got a scheme. "They'll git us, but maybe they'll be consid'rable disapp'inted about the t-t-t—"

"Turbine," says I. "How so? If they git to the cave they'll have it, won't they?"

"It looks that way," says he, "but you never can tell."

I got up and looked inside. There, covered up with the sheets, was the engine, so I knew Mark was only talking to encourage me.

Batten and Bill stood up and faced around to us so we could see what they had been making.

"There!" says Mark. "What'd I tell you?"

Sure enough. They had made shelters out of those willow branches. Not shields, but just big green bundles tied together with handkerchiefs and string. They were so big that when Batten and Bill held them up nothing but their feet showed.

Right off they started up the hill. The attack commenced.

"Shoot," says Mark, "and keep on shootin'."

"You bet!" I whispered to myself.

The enemy looked like two walking brush-heaps. Honest, it was kind of funny to see them crawling up-hill, and then, on the other hand, it wasn't comical at all, for there was no stopping them. The minute they stepped into range we began firing, but our pebbles spatted against the shields and didn't do a bit of harm. Once in a while we managed to clip Batten on the leg or Bill on the arm, but that was all.

On they came, slow as snails, but getting nearer and nearer. We peppered at them as fast as we could set stones in our slings, but we might as well have been shooting into the river with the idea of hitting a fish. They meant business, too; you could tell it by the way they kept coming without saying a word, grim-like. I began to shake in the knees, but Mark was as steady as a tree. I was willing to give up and scoot, but he never budged, just drew back his rubbers and whanged away as if he was shooting at a target. Cool! He was so cool the breeze across him got chilly.

Now the enemy was only sixty feet down, now fifty, now forty. Up, up they came, closer and closer. We could hear them panting, and the sound of their hands clutching and their feet crunching into the bank. Once in a while the loose earth would give away and one of them would slip back a few feet. The only good that did was, maybe, to give us a shot back at the shield. You can be good and sure we never let a chance slip.

Thirty feet! Twenty-five feet! Twenty feet! The nearer they came the louder my heart beat and the more my knees wabbled. I know how a soldier feels just before he turns and runs—and I know why he doesn't turn and run: it's because the soldier next to him doesn't; it's because he's ashamed to have the other soldiers think he's more afraid than they are. Mark showed no more signs of running than a saw horse, so I stayed on.

All the time I'd been saving up one last hope. When Batten and Bill were scrambling onto the shelf in front of the cave I turned and hauled myself up the slope to my big boulder where I'd left the lever.

"Git to one side, Mark!" I yelled.

He edged over ten feet to the right. Bill and Batten kept right on. The cave was under their noses, and the turbine was in the cave. That was all they thought of right then, I guess. They were going to get it back! They had lost it after all their trouble, and now they were going to get it again. Neither of them offered to bother Mark; they made straight for the cave and the engine.

"Look out below!" I shouted.

They looked up and stopped sudden, so sudden they almost toppled over backward.

"Keep away from the cave," says I, "or I'll push the stone over!"

Batten scowled like he'd have been glad to bite me. "You get away from there. Drop that lever and come down here!"

"I'll drop nothin'," says I, "unless it's this stone onto your head."

I never would have dared to push it over on them, even to save the engine. I don't believe any boy would. But Batten didn't know as much about boys as I did, and the boulder looked mighty dangerous from below. They stood right where they were.

"We'll get you," says Bill; and he started to go around and come up after me. Batten went the other way so they could take me on both sides at once. I waited until they were almost reaching out for me, and then I toppled over the stone. It wasn't with any idea of hitting them, for they were out of line, but it did seem to me we might gain a few minutes' time if the boulder would drop in front of the door of the cave and stick so they'd have to move it before they could get in. Every minute was valuable now, for it was past noon, and help *must* be on the way.

When I toppled the stone I jumped after it and struck in the soft sand on all fours. The boulder had slipped down, gouging a groove out of the face of the hill, and stopped right in front of the door! It had fallen so straight, and the sand was so soft, it hadn't rolled a mite—just sunk in about six inches and closed up the lower part of the entrance to the cave. There was a foot or so of room above, but it would be hard for a big man to squeeze through, and impossible to get the turbine out until it was moved away.

Mark stood over at the side, looking at me surprised.

"Tallow," says he, "that was a b-b-bully idee!"

"Here they come," I says.

Batten and Bill didn't lose any time, but slid back to the shelf. When they saw the stone they talked about it quite a bit and not polite. It tickled me to hear how mad they were.

"Wait," says Batten to me, "till we get the engine out, and we'll look after you."

"I won't be here," says I. "Good-by!"

I started to get up and go away from there, but Mark whispers: "Wait a minute. Don't run yet."

Batten and Bill puffed and hauled and sweated rolling the stone out of the way. It took them five minutes to make a clear way, and you'd better believe it was no easy job. All tired out as they were, they rushed into the cave without waiting to rest. I heard Mark make a funny noise in his throat, but his face was sober as a Sunday-school superintendent's.

I looked in after the men. Batten jumped for the covered engine and jerked the sheet off. Well, sir, I just fell backward onto the sand. I couldn't believe what I saw, for under the sheet was nothing in the world but a heap of dry boughs. The engine was gone!

Batten and Bill stood like they were frozen solid, their mouths open. Then Batten made a noise that sounded between a roar and a growl and kicked the brush-pile.

"It ain't there," says Bill.

Batten rushed out of the cave, almost bumping his head on the roof, and pounced on me. He took me by the collar and shook me. "Where is it?" he yelled. "Where is it?"

I felt of my neck to see if it was all there, and then answered him, sort of strangled:

"I dunno. I thought it was there."

He looked at me, and I guess the surprise was still plain on my face. "I thought it was there," I said again. "Honest!"

"Did that Indian take it with him?"

"Not that I know of," I says.

Bill broke in then. "It must be here somewhere, or they wouldn't have stayed around to fight. What did they try to keep us out for?"

That was what I wanted to know. If Mark knew the engine was gone, why did he stay around instead of making for home? I couldn't understand.

"Maybe there's a hiding-place in there," Bill said.

They both hurried into the cave again and poked all around, hunting for another opening and prodding the floor to see if we had buried the turbine. Of course they couldn't find anything, because there wasn't anything there.

Out they came again.

"That fat kid knows, *I'll* bet," says Bill.

They looked around for him and so did I, but he was gone.

CHAPTER XX

I didn't know what to make of it. Mark wasn't the kind of er fellow to run away and leave me to face Batten and Bill; but, all the same, he was gone. Not a sign could we see. He must have sneaked off while the men were looking for the engine in the cave. One thing I was sure of, he hadn't carried the turbine away with him. Maybe both of us together could have lifted it, but we certainly couldn't have carried it up the hill.

I reached down and pinched myself to see if I was awake. There was getting to be so many mysteries and disappearances and such-like that it got to seeming like a dream where things pop in and out without any reason or excuse. But it wasn't a dream, for there was Batten and Bill, scowling as ferocious as a couple of wolves. (I never saw a wolf scowl, but if he does it must be ferocious.) No, sir, it wasn't any dream—not a bit of it. What I remembered about getting back the turbine, and the night on the rattlesnake island, and getting the turbine up-hill to the cave really happened. The engine had been in the cave, because I helped put it there. According to what I figured out, it must be there yet. It couldn't have gotten out. But it *was* out! When a thing happens that you know positively can't happen it sort of shakes you up. It made me feel pretty creepy.

I had been around the cave ever since we put the turbine in, except for the little while I was spying on Batten and Bill when they almost caught me; and Mark had been sitting right before the door all of that time. Nobody could have taken it out without his seeing it, and he hadn't said a word to me about anything happening while I was gone. It was too much for me. One thing I knew, though, and that was that the only time that engine could have gotten away was while I was gone. The only reasonable way to explain it was that Mark had carried it away; but, then, Mark couldn't have lifted it alone. And there you are! What would anybody expect a fellow to make of such a mess?

Batten came and stood over me, threatening-like. "Boy," says he, "where's that engine?"

"Mr. Batten," says I (I thought it was best to be sort of polite), "I wish I knew."

"It was in that cave, wasn't it?"

"Yes," says I; "it was in there, all right, and how it ever got out beats me."

"Do you mean to say you didn't know it was gone?"

"Honest, Mr. Batten," says I, "I thought it was there till you yanked off the sheets."

He turned to Bill. "What do you think of it?" he asked. "Is the kid telling the truth?"

"If he ain't," says Bill, "he's a good one. I never see a kid look more like he *was* tellin' the truth."

"Who's been around here besides you two boys?"

"Nobody I know of," I told him, "except you two."

"Cross your heart," says he; "haven't you seen anybody else?"

"Not a soul," I says, and made a cross-mark over the front of me.

"If that engine ever was in the cave," Bill put in, "it must be somewheres around here. It was there when we came, and it can't have got away far. We've been watchin' perty careful, you know."

"That's right. It would have been mighty hard to cart it off without our seeing them. But it's gone, just the same," he says.

"What's these things?" Bill asked me, kicking at the lengths of sapling Mark had cut. They were about two feet long and there were three or four of them.

"I dunno," I told him. "Maybe Mark cut them for a fire."

"Um!" says Bill, dubious-like. "Let's skirmish around some, Batten. If I ain't mistaken that engine is hid close to here."

They started looking for it, and, seeing they didn't act like they were going to damage me any, I hung around to see what they'd find. They went poking down holes and looking under brush-heaps and in the middle of clumps of bushes, but not a hide or hair of the turbine did they run onto. They searched and searched and searched, careful, as if they were looking for a nickel in a pile of sand. They started near the cave, and worked away in circles, and there wasn't an inch they didn't hunt over.

All at once I heard Mark holler, and when I looked up there he stood, with Uncle Ike Bond right beside him. Batten and Bill looked, too, and they didn't wait to chat with Uncle Ike; they legged it down to the boat as fast as they could hike and shoved off. I couldn't resist scooting a couple of pebbles after them, but they were in such a hurry I didn't hit either time. I turned and yelled to Uncle Ike.

"You didn't come any too soon," I said.

Uncle Ike was mad clean through and came plunging down to the cave a lot more rapid than an old gentleman ought to move. "The scalawags!" says he. "The scamps—the—what-d'ye-call-'ems! Pickin' on a passel of boys like you! I'd like to lay my buggy-whip acrost their shoulders, I would. Maybe they wouldn't dance! Maybe! They seen me, though, and they won't be back—not them. Not where old Uncle Bond can git holt of 'em. They're gone for good."

"Looks that way," says Mark.

"Peddler give me your knife," Uncle Ike says. "He didn't find me till about fifteen minutes ago. I knowed there wa'n't no foolin' about it, so I come a-peltin'.

Smart thing, sendin' that knife; mighty smart. In all the years I've drove a bus I hain't seen nothin' smarter. Your pa, Tallow, and Mr. Whiteley is comin' behind. Couldn't keep up with me, not them."

"We're awful glad you're here," Mark says. And Uncle Ike jerked his head like he was glad, too, and pretty proud of himself.

"Your father's home," says he to Mark. "Got home this mornin' and found you gone and the engine gone. It most set him crazy. Never see a man so flustered. Didn't know what to do, not him, so what does he up and go at? Why, he grabs that there *Decline and Fall of the Roman Empire* and goes to readin' it to see if it won't tell him how to act. Says he to me, 'Mr. Bond, it's in this here book if I can find it. Everythin's in this book.' And your mother, she jest walked up and down and couldn't say a word, she was that scairt. What ever possessed you to go prowlin' off without sayin' a word?"

"We didn't have no time to tell anybody. And we didn't want ma to know the turbine was stole," says Mark.

Well, pretty soon along came my father and Mr. Whiteley, excited as could be and perspiring so their collars were melted. Dad he grabbed onto me and says: "What does this mean, young man? Where have you been? You've been scaring your mother and me most to death."

"We—we went to get back Mr. Tidd's engine," I said, kind of shaky.

"Pretty pickle," snapped Mr. Whiteley, "standing the town on its head. You ought to be ashamed of yourselves."

"If you'd had the sense of a pint of mice," says my father, "you'd have known a couple of kids couldn't do any good. Why didn't you come right off and tell me?"

"Didn't think of it," I says; and that was true, too.

"Now see what comes of being headstrong," says Mr. Whiteley. "Probably the engine is gone for good. The men that took it have got a whole day's start. If you'd come to us right away there wouldn't have been much trouble getting it back. What you need is a good belting, both of you."

"I'll look after that, Whiteley," says my father; "don't ever worry."

Now that was a nice thing, wasn't it? After what Mark and I had gone through, to get licked for it! Seems like grownup folks are mighty unreasonable sometimes.

"I guess maybe," says Mark to Mr. Whiteley, "we'll git back the t-t-t—"

"Turbine," says I.

"Turbine," he says, "after all—"

"Bosh!" says Mr. Whiteley. "The men have disappeared, and the engine with them."

Mark pointed off across the river where Batten and Bill were landing out of their boat. "There they go," he said, "and they ain't got the turbine with them that I can see."

Uncle Ike was grinning as hard as he could grin, and looking at Mr. Whiteley out of the corner of his eye.

"What's that? What's that?" my father asks.

"It's Henry C. Batten and Bill," says Mark, "and the turbine—well, you come along with me. I g-guess maybe we'll find it."

Uncle Ike roared out loud and slapped Mr. Whiteley on the back. "I told you," says he. "Slicker'n greased lightnin'. Yes, sir, you can't git ahead of that boy—him with his signs and signals and what-not."

"Mark," says I, in a whisper, "the turbine's gone."

He looked at me kind of blank a minute and then grinned.

"Gone, is it?" says he. "Kind of lucky it was gone, too, wasn't it? Eh?" He looked awful self-satisfied, and it kind of roiled me.

"Well?" says Mr. Whiteley, pretty impatient. "Well?"

"Come on," says Mark. He led them to the cave and pointed in. "We got it back," says he, "and put it in there. Then along came those men, chasin' after us, and we had to fight them off. I was sure they'd beat us sooner or later and git back the engine, so when Tallow was off scoutin' I hid it."

"Um!" says I. "How?"

"Easy," says he. "I cut some rollers to put under it and tied a rope around it. It wasn't hard to haul it along then. All I did was to drag it out to the edge of that gully"—he pointed—"and let it over the edge slow, hangin' onto the rope so it wouldn't slip." That was what those lengths of sapling were.

We walked over and looked into the washout, but there wasn't any engine; nothing but a heap of rocks.

"It's under there," says Mark. "I piled those stones over it as careful as could be, and then s-s-smoothed out the sand so nobody could tell I'd been around there. And there's your engine!"

Father and Mr. Whiteley couldn't say very much after that, but they kept on being stern out of principle, like grown folks do. They had to thaw out some, though.

"How'd you do it?" Uncle Ike wanted to know.

"They can tell us goin' back," says Mr. Whiteley. "Mr. and Mrs. Tidd don't know they're found yet."

Together we got the turbine out and up the hill and onto Uncle Ike's wagon. Then we set out for town.

"Your father came home unexpectedly early this morning," Mr. Whiteley told Mark "and he's all upset about losing his invention and you, too."

"What made him come home so quick?" Mark asked.

"Lost his money," says Mr. Whiteley, grinning a little. "Telegraphed me last night so as not to frighten your mother. Here's his telegram."

The telegram said:

Money lost. Can't pay hotel bill. Can't pay anything. What shall I do?

Now wasn't that just like Mr. Tidd? Well, Mr. Whiteley telegraphed him back some money, and he took the first train home. Said he wasn't going to take any more chances in the city.

"Did he get his p-p-patent?" Mark asked.

"He didn't get anything but flabbergasted," says Mr. Whiteley. "And when he got here and found what had happened he was more flabbergasted than ever."

Uncle Ike slapped his knee. "That reminds me," says he. "I took a perty slick-lookin' feller up to see him just before that peddler give me your knife. He was a feller with a shiny leather bag and a plug hat and glasses that pinched onto his nose and whiskers. He looked like he was so loaded down with ten-dollar gold pieces he couldn't walk. He was one of them pompous fellers. Strutted around like a turkey in a yard full of banty chickens."

Mark looked up sharp. "What was his name?" he asked.

"Dunno," says Uncle Ike. "He didn't say. Just come a-struttin' up to me and says, 'My good man, can you take me to the house of a man named Tidd immediately?' I looked him in the eye and says back: 'My good man, I kin take you there, and I kin take you immediate, or I kin take you less immediate. It all depends.' Well, he got in without sayin' any more, and I charged him double fare. He's there now."

"Uncle Ike," says Mark, with his mouth set firm and his eyes twinkling bright, "can you make these horses git?"

"I kin," says Uncle Ike, "if it's necessary."

"It's mighty necessary," says Mark.

Uncle Ike leaned over and laid his whip across the horses' back. "Giddap, there!" he yelled, and off we went, rocking and rattling and jumping and tipping down the road toward Wicksville.

CHAPTER XXI

Mark Tidd's father was walking up and down the parlor with a volume of the *Decline and Fall* in his hand when the pompous man with the silk hat rapped at the door. Mr. Tidd would read a few lines and then go stamping across the floor, shaking his head and talking to himself as though he'd lost his mind. His hair, what there was of it, was all rumpled up, and he was so excited and afraid and fidgety he couldn't keep still.

Mrs. Tidd was out cleaning up in the kitchen. That was just like her; she would have to go on working if a cyclone came and blew away the front of the house. Yes, sir, she'd keep right on scrubbing what was left.

The man with the silk hat pounded on the door two or three times before anybody heard him, but at last Mr. Tidd went poking out and opened the door a crack.

"Is this Mr. Tidd?" the man asked.

Mr. Tidd nodded, but didn't say anything, because he didn't think of anything to say.

"I," says the man, "am Hamilton Carver, attorney for the International Engineering Company."

"Oh," Mr. Tidd says, in a dull sort of way, "be you?"

"Yes, sir." Carver blew out his chest and looked important. "I came from Pittsburg to have a talk with you, sir."

"From Pittsburg?" says Mr. Tidd. "From Pittsburg, eh? To talk with me? Um! Well, mister, there ain't anything I want to talk about to-day. No, sir, not a thing."

"But I have something I want to talk with you about, and it'll be very much to your advantage to listen to me."

"I don't know what to do," Mr. Tidd says, mostly to himself. "My son's gone, and my turbine's gone—everything's gone. I've read the *Decline and Fall*, mister, for two hours. Two hours! But it hain't helped none. I wisht I knew what to do."

"May I come in?" asked the lawyer.

"Come in," says Mr. Tidd, "and sit."

They went into the parlor, where Carver sat down; but Mr. Tidd went right on pacing up and down as if he was all alone, reading away at the *Decline and Fall*, and mumbling, and shaking his head, and tugging away at his ear.

"I came," says Carver, "to see you about your invention. I have been sent to negotiate with you—to—er—endeavor to enter into an—er—business arrangement with you."

"Oh," says Mr. Tidd. "Um!"

"Your invention may be valuable, and it may be worthless," Carver went on.

But Mr. Tidd broke in, cross-like: "It ain't worthless. It's goin' to—to revolutionize transportation, mister. It's been tested; yes, sir, tested. No guess-work. It does what I said it would do. I know. But it's been stole."

Carver's eyes twinkled, and he smiled to himself as if he was pretty well satisfied with something.

"You seem worried," says he. "Maybe I can help clear things up for you."

"Somebody's run off with my model—night before last. Gone. Take six months to make another."

"You're in a pretty bad way, then, if they should go and get a patent on it, aren't you? Looks as though you wouldn't have a chance, doesn't it?"

"Bad—it looks perty bad! I've thought and I've figgered. Readin' the *Decline and Fall* don't help none. First time it ever failed me. And my boy's gone, too."

"It's fortunate I came, then," says the lawyer. "I will be willing to make you an offer for your invention even under the circumstances. I can help you that much. Not a big offer, maybe, but a good offer, considering."

"It ain't no good with the model gone," says Tidd, shaking his head despondent-like.

"My company will be willing to take the risk. What would you say if I was to offer to buy your invention and take all the worry right off your hands?"

"I dunno," says Mr. Tidd. "I dunno what I would say."

"I've got a paper here all drawn up. It's an assignment of your rights, properly executed. You understand? A sort of deed, you know. Now the chances are you will never see your model again and that you won't get a cent out of it. But we are willing to pay you something. It's the only way you'll ever get a penny."

"Maybe so," said Mr. Tidd. "I'm sort of confused to-day. Mark's gone, and the turbine's gone, and I can't think very clear."

"Whatever we pay you will be just that much you wouldn't get if you don't sell to us. Be a sensible man, now, and make the best of things. You've lost your machine. The wise thing to do is to get as much as you can and forget all about it. Go to inventing something else."

"I sha'n't ever invent anything else," Mr. Tidd says, almost in a whisper.

Carver reached into his pocket and pulled out a big roll of bills. "See there," he said. "I've got the money right in my hand." He shook it in the air so the bills crinkled and crackled. "Remember, you'll never have another chance. If you don't sell to me now you'll never get anything."

"How much be you offerin'?"

"I'll give you—five hundred dollars."

Mr. Tidd shook his head slow and worried. "Don't seem like that was enough. No, sir, that don't seem enough nohow."

"Well, I'll stretch a point. Just sign your name to this assignment and I'll give you seven hundred and fifty."

Mr. Tidd walked to the table and took the fountain-pen the lawyer offered him. He held it in his hand and looked out of the window with tears standing in his eyes. "An' I figgered it would make me rich. Seven hundred and fifty dollars. Oh, ho! Mister, it's cost me more'n that to make the model. Oh, ho!"

"Sign right there," said Carver, pointing to a line.

"Maybe I better speak to my wife about it first," Mr. Tidd said, not being certain what he ought to do. I guess he didn't really know just what he *was* doing.

"Nonsense," the lawyer put in, quick. "Just sign right there, and the money's yours. It's just getting that much you never would get any other way."

"I s'pose maybe so," Mr. Tidd says, and drew up a chair to sign. The lawyer sat back and sort of held his breath until Mr. Tidd's name should be written on his paper. Mr. Tidd looked at the pen, shook it a little, and leaned over the table. He made the first letter of his name when there was a whopping racket on the porch and Mark came running slam-bang into the house.

"D-d-dad!" he yelled. "Dad!"

Mr. Tidd looked up and then heaved a big sigh.

"Marcus," he said, "you're all right!"

Mark didn't pay any attention. "Have you taken any money?" he said. "Have you s-s-signed anythin'?"

"I'm just a-goin' to," says Mr. Tidd. "I'm a-gittin' what I kin. The engine's gone—lost! I'm gittin' what I kin."

Well, Mark just reached for that paper and mussed it all up in his hand. He was so mad his fat cheeks shook. "You," says he to Carver, "git right out of here! G-g-git!"

"Marcus," says his father, in that mild way of his.

"He's tryin' to cheat you. He's in with Batten and them folks."

Uncle Ike and Mr. Whiteley and dad and I were all standing in the hall. Now Mr. Whiteley stepped into the room.

"I don't know who you are," says he to the lawyer, "but if you know what's good for you you'll take the first train out of town."

"YOU GIT RIGHT OUT OF HERE! G-G-GIT!"

"But," says Mr. Tidd, "but my turbine's gone, and he'll give me seven hundred—"

"Your turbine ain't gone," says Mark, stuttering so he could hardly speak. "It's out in the wagon right this m-m-m—"

"Minute," I says, to help him out.

The lawyer got up and edged around to the door. He didn't say a word, but put on his hat and went out of the house quick; and that was the end of *him*.

Mr. Tidd sat like he was stunned, not knowing exactly what had happened, and turning from one to the other of us with the blankest look you ever saw.

"But," says he, "what—"

Mr. Whiteley turned in then and told him the whole business. As he went along describing how Mark and I had gone after the engine Mr. Tidd kept looking at Mark and blinking; and pretty soon he stretched out his hand and took a hold of Mark and pulled him over close, hanging onto him tight. When Mr. Whiteley told about the way we stood the siege at the cave and fought Batten and Bill Mr. Tidd patted Mark soft-like with his hand and looked up at him that proud you'd never believe it. I felt funny to see him sitting there so kind of honest and simple and good. My throat ached and—well, I walked over and made believe I was looking out of the window.

When Mr. Whiteley was all done Mr. Tidd says, kind of choked up and broken; "I never heard anything like it—never. Man and boy I've been a-readin' the *Decline and Fall* thirty-five years, and there ain't a thing in it equal to this. Not a thing. No, sir."

We didn't stay very long after that, but went away and left Mark with his father and mother and the turbine. I never saw three folks so happy as they were, and I never saw two people as proud of a boy as Mr. and Mrs. Tidd were of Mark. And I don't blame them.

Plunk and Binney and I weren't long getting together, and as soon as we thought it was polite we went hurrying over to Mark's. Plunk and Binney wanted to hear all about it again, and to have Mark do the telling. We felt it was the biggest thing that ever happened in Wicksville, and I can tell you we were pretty proud to be mixed up in it. The town was all excited, and folks kept coming to call on Mrs. Tidd in a steady stream until she was so nervous and flustered it wasn't safe for us boys to stay around. Mrs. Tidd was the kind of person that wanted to do her regular work every day, no matter what happened; and she didn't have a speck of patience with all the inquisitive folks that came traipsing over to ask about it, and get a look at Mark as though they hadn't been seeing him every day for almost a year. She kept getting sharper and sharper, and more anxious and more anxious to get to her work, until Mark says to us that we'd better dig out before the explosion came.

"She can't take it out on the folks," says he, "so we'll catch it. Somebody's b-b-bound to."

We went off down-town. Mark suggested it. I guess he wanted to give the people a chance to look at him. He was a great fellow that way, and always wanted all the glory that could be got out of anything. I don't know as there is anything funny about that, because I sort of liked to have men stop when we went past and whisper and point after us; and it was all right to have other kids you knew stand back, awed-like, and watch you as if you had just come back from the middle of Africa. I tell you we were some folks, Mark and me.

All that day we loafed around and told the story. I wish it could have lasted always, for we were treated like we were all Presidents of the United States come on a visit. Folks were so good to us that I was sick that night. It was that way everywhere we went. The grocer called us in to tell him about it, and told us to help ourselves; there was a crowd in the drug store, and Smiley set out a dish of candy. Everywhere we ate and ate and ate, which was all right for Mark, because he was used to it and had room to put it all; but after a while I got full and couldn't cram down another thing. It was enough to make a fellow mad, with all sorts of things to eat and no place to put them.

Uncle Ike was quite a hero, too. He told his part of it a hundred times, and got us to ride back and forth in his bus with him just to show how intimate we were. He was a little jealous of Zadok Biggs, but Biggs was so good-natured and so full of admiration for Mark that Uncle Ike couldn't get up a grudge; and before night they were friends for life, as Zadok would say.

The story spread around the country, and in the afternoon farmers began coming in. Of course, they had excuses for coming, but we knew, and everybody else knew, they just came to see us and hear all about it. I guess there isn't a more curious and inquiring part of the country than ours.

With all of it we were pretty tired by night, and pretty well satisfied with ourselves, too. Who wouldn't be? Hadn't we really done something? And didn't the people show they were proud of us? Well, then, why shouldn't we be swelled up a little?

Once, early in the day, some of the men talked about getting up a crowd and going after Henry C. Batten and Bill; but they didn't make a go of it, and it isn't likely they would have caught them, anyhow.

On the way home to supper we met Zadok Biggs on his wagon. He stopped and called to us.

"Marcus Aurelius," says he, "it is my desire—wish—to meet your parents. I shall consider it an honor and a distinction. I shall go with you and meet your parents—the parents of Marcus Aurelius Fortunatus Tidd!"

"Come on," says Mark, "and stay to supper." He knew his mother would be glad to have Zadok to a meal so she could thank him a lot for helping him out and so she could ask him a heap of questions. Dad had already said I could go to Mark's, so we'd be all in a crowd together. Zadok made room for us on the seat— that is, he made most room enough for Mark, and I sat on top of the wagon. And so we drove to Tidd's.

"Where've you been all day? That's what I'd like to know," snapped Mrs. Tidd, when we came to the door. She didn't see there was company, or she wouldn't have lit into Mark till they were alone. But Zadok stepped from behind and bowed way over, and Mark introduced him.

"Sakes alive!" says Mrs. Tidd. "Sakes alive!" And she kept looking and looking at Zadok like he was a curiosity out of a sideshow—which he pretty nearly was. Then she remembered her manners and asked us to come in.

"Madam," says Zadok, "you have a son to be proud of. And he, Marcus Aurelius, has parents that in turn he may well boast about. His name, Mrs. Tidd, attracted me to him. I knew that one with such a name must be out of the ordinary run, and so it proved. He's a remarkable boy, ma'am."

Mrs. Tidd blushed and looked at Mark out of the corner of her eye as proud as a hen with eleven chickens.

"I won't go as far's to say he's a *bad* boy, Mr. Biggs. He's been well spoke of, though he is a trial, what with his mischief and his appetite. But there's worse boys in Wicksville!" Here she looked at me, and I looked out of the window. Maybe she didn't mean anything that time, but mostly she did.

Mrs. Tidd went to the back door and called Mr. Tidd, who was out in his workshop fussing with his turbine. It seemed he was so glad to get it back he couldn't leave it alone a minute. But he came in to supper because he knew his wife would come out and make him whether he wanted to or not.

"Dad," says Mark, "this is Mr. Zadok Biggs. If it hadn't been for him Tallow and I never would have got the engine back safe."

Mr. Tidd shook hands with Zadok, so there couldn't be any doubt what he thought. As for Zadok, he stood off and bowed to Mr. Tidd with his hand on his stomach.

"Mr. Tidd," says he, "it was you, I understand, who gave the remarkable, the admirable name of Marcus Aurelius Fortunatus to your son. It was an achievement, sir. Beside it even the Tidd turbine is insignificant—some folks would say small. I congratulate you, sir."

"It ain't such a bad name," agreed Mr. Tidd, pretty well pleased.

"Bad, sir! It is stupendous—no less. But, my friends, let us consider business. How have you succeeded, Mr. Tidd, with your affairs in the city?"

"I don't understand much about it," said Mr. Tidd, looking kind of bewildered. "The lawyer did a pile of talking and wrote a lot of papers and things, but just what it all amounted to I'm blessed as I can see. He didn't give me no patent. I came home before he was through."

Zadok Biggs blinked. For quite a while Zadok kept staring and blinking at Mr. Tidd as though he didn't know what to make of it. Sometimes he looked mad, sometimes he looked disappointed, and sometimes he looked just plain flabbergasted. Then, all of a sudden, his face looked relieved, and he let a twinkle come into his eye. He nudged Mark with his elbow.

"Genius," says he, "that's it. Your father's a genius, Marcus Aurelius. For a minute I was disappointed. I admit it. I thought maybe giving you your name was just chance, but now I see how it was. It was another side to the genius that invented the turbine. Ah, ah! Your father, Marcus, is not clever on the financial side—not a good business man, is the plainer way to say it. And, Marcus, listen to me. Listen to Zadok Biggs. The turbine isn't safe yet, and it won't be safe after the patent issues. No, sir. But Zadok Biggs is your friend for life. I will assume the business responsibility."

Mark didn't quite follow him. All he understood clear was that the turbine was still in danger.

"How is it in danger?" he wanted to know.

"Your father will get cheated out of his rights yet. Many inventors have. What good, I ask you, is his invention until the turbines are manufactured and sold? That requires money. The man who contributes—gives—the money will cheat him. It would be as easy as—as cracking an egg with a sledge-hammer."

Mark knew it, and it worried him a heap. No matter how close they watched his father, there was no telling when somebody might get hold of him and gouge his patent out of him while he sat with his eyes wide open looking on. There wasn't anything in the *Decline and Fall* about patents or business, and outside of mechanics the *Decline and Fall* was about all the real experience Mr. Tidd had.

That afternoon Zadok Biggs drove away on his wagon. He never could stay very long in one place because, he said, he had a disease that he called the wandering foot, and it kept him moving. The last thing he said to Mark as he shook the lines on Rosinante's back was; "Don't let your pa do anything—*anything* about that turbine till you hear from me. I've written a letter. I, Zadok Biggs, have written an important letter. Until I get a communication in return—reply, you would say—don't let him do a thing."

Mark promised he'd look after things careful and we stood waving our hands to Zadok as long as his red wagon was in sight.

Every day after that we went to the post-office to see if there was a letter from him, but we didn't hear a word. A whole week went by, and we didn't get so much as a postal to tell us where he was.

"He's gone off and forgot all about us," I told Mark.

"Not him," says Mark. "He jest hain't got around to do what he wanted to, that's all. We'll be hearin' from him perty quick. D-d-don't you worry."

Well, it wasn't any of my funeral, so I didn't argue with him!

CHAPTER XXII

Next morning Mark got a telegram from Zadok Biggs. It's quite a thing for a boy to get a real telegram, and he was puffed up over it considerable, showing it to me and Plunk and Binney as if it was a diamond stole out of an idol's eye, or some such precious thing as that. It said:

> Marcus Aurelius Fortunatus Tidd,—Coming. Hold the fort. Shoo 'em away. News. Friend for life.
>
> Zadok Biggs.

We couldn't make much out of it except that he was coming, so we waited for him to turn up, which he did late that afternoon. He drove up the alley whistling "Marching through Georgia," and left his red wagon back of Mr. Tidd's barn-workshop while he turned Rosinante loose in the back yard to eat the grass and Mrs. Tidd's vegetable garden. We hustled out to meet him.

"Ah!" says he. "My friend, Marcus Aurelius, and his friends awaiting me, so to speak, with eagerness, eh? I telegraphed. Couldn't wait." He was fairly jumping up and down with excitement, and his long, lean face was almost glittering, he was so happy. "I said I would look after the business matters. I, Zadok Biggs, said so. And I *have* looked after them. I have news for you."

"W-won't you c-c-come in?" Mark asked, when he got a chance.

"Of course. Certainly. To meet your esteemed father, the man of genius, who bestowed upon—gave—you your name, and who, as a secondary example of his genius, invented the Tidd turbine." He came trotting after Mark, and we followed him. It was a funny sight to see Mark waddling along, big as a hippopotamus, and Zadok trotting after with little short steps sort of like a playful puppy.

Mr. Tidd was sitting in the kitchen, with the *Decline and Fall* open on his lap, watching his wife thumb a pie around the edge. He looked up when we came in, and then got onto his feet.

"F-f-father," says Mark, "here is Zadok B-b-biggs again."

"Um!" says Mr. Tidd, looking at Zadok like he was some peculiar kind of a bug and he didn't know whether to be afraid of him or not. "Um! Zadok Biggs. Howdy do, Mr. Biggs. Howdy do."

Zadok grabbed hold of his hand and shook it like he was pumping water on a cold morning. "Mr. Tidd," says he, "this is a proud minute. I, Zadok Biggs, swell with pride to clasp your hand, the hand that named Marcus Aurelius Fortunatus."

"And," Mrs. Tidd put in, "the hand that hain't never spanked him in the way he deserved."

"Mrs. Tidd," says Zadok, "do you recall my promise? You do. Of course you do. I said I would look after the financial aspects—business side is perhaps the more usual expression—of the Tidd turbine. Did I not? Of course I did. Well, madam and sir, my friends, I have looked after it. Did Zadok Biggs let grass grow under his feet? No. Behold!"

He drew a letter out of his pocket and waved it in the air. "From William Abbott," he said. "Yes, my friends, from William Abbott. Know him? No? Ah! We went to school together. Zadok Biggs and William Abbott, schoolmates. Now look at us. William, a millionaire; Zadok, a tin-peddler. Life is strange."

Mrs. Tidd was wiping her hands on her apron, and Mr. Tidd was thumbing over the *Decline and Fall* with a bewildered look on his face. "Yes," says she. "But what about it? What's in the letter?"

"Of course. Natural question; and I, Zadok Biggs, will answer it. I communicated—wrote—on account of the Tidd turbine to him. I described it. I discussed the merits of the invention, not forgetting the genius of the inventor. And he has replied. He is interested. In short, my friends, through the instrumentality of Zadok Biggs he is coming to Wicksville, and for no other purpose than to look into this matter. Wonderful? No, not at all."

"W-when's he c-c-comin'?" asked Mark.

"Natural question, again. William Abbott, millionaire, will arrive—be here— on the six-o'clock train. We will await him. Mrs. Tidd will greet him with a piece of that pie, eh? A large piece. It will delight him."

We all went into the parlor and waited. Mrs. Tidd made us go into that room because she thought it was the most fitting place to receive a millionaire. Well, sure enough, before half past six up drove Uncle Ike's bus, and out got a big man, 'most as big as Sammy, but dressed kind of careless, with an old slouch hat on. I was disappointed. I'd expected to see a fellow all over diamonds, with one of those coats cut out in the front so all the shirt showed, and a plug hat. But he wasn't that way at all; he might have owned a grocery store for all you could tell by the looks of him.

Zadok rushed out to meet him, and they shook hands cordial. Mr. Abbott was tickled to see Zadok, that was plain; and Zadok was tickled to see Mr. Abbott. They came into the parlor, and every one of us was introduced. He was a fine man, no frills and no fuss. I'd like to take him fishing.

He was sort of bashful at first, I guess, but pretty soon he had us boys talking baseball and things, and we were all laughing and having the best sort of a time.

"I was invited to supper," he says to Mrs. Tidd, "and I've been looking forward to it, I can tell you. Zadok wrote about your pies. We're going to have pie, aren't we?" He seemed to be mighty anxious about it till he found out we were.

It was a dandy meal. When it was all done we went back into the parlor to talk business. Mr. Abbott and Zadok did all the talking, and the rest of us just looked on. Before bedtime the whole thing was settled, and Mr. Tidd was going to be a rich man. Mr. Abbott was going to manufacture and sell the Tidd turbine, and Mr. Tidd was going to get what they called a royalty. That means he was going to get a certain amount of money for every one that was sold.

"Of course," said Mr. Abbott, "this is provided the turbine does what you say it will do. I haven't seen it, you know, and am depending wholly on what Zadok Biggs here has told me."

"It'll w-w-w-work," says Mark. "I s-seen it."

Mr. Abbott laughed and said he was sure it *would* work; and then we fellows went home, and the Tidds and Zadok and Mr. Abbott went to bed.

Next day the turbine was set up and tested again in Mr. Whiteley's machine shop, and all the papers were signed.

That's about the end of the story of Marcus Aurelius Fortunatus Tidd and the turbine. But you might as well know that the invention was a great success. Mr. Tidd did get rich. Money came in so fast he didn't know what to do with it, so he just let Mr. Abbott look after it for him.

It was a good thing for every one of us boys, because Mr. Tidd said we had helped so much he had to do something for us; and next year, when we're through high school, he's going to send the whole four of us to college together.

And Sammy? Mr. Tidd fixed it up with the poor-farm so Sammy won't be disturbed, but can go all over whenever he wants to. And there's no danger of his going hungry or wanting anything as long as he lives.

Uncle Ike keeps right on driving the bus, because that's the thing he enjoys the most—says it's interesting and instructive. He told me it was a better education than going to college, but I don't put much stock in that.

And there you are! Taking it all together, we had quite a time of it, and lots of excitement, and every bit of it was due, just as I prophesied, to having a fat boy that stuttered in town.

THE END

Lector House believes that a society develops through a two-fold approach of continuous learning and adaptation, which is derived from the study of classic literary works spread across the historic timeline of literature records. Therefore, we aim at reviving, repairing and redeveloping all those inaccessible or damaged but historically as well as culturally important literature across subjects so that the future generations may have an opportunity to study and learn from past works to embark upon a journey of creating a better future.

This book is a result of an effort made by Lector House towards making a contribution to the preservation and repair of original ancient works which might hold historical significance to the approach of continuous learning across subjects.

HAPPY READING & LEARNING!

LECTOR HOUSE
LECTOR HOUSE LLP
E-MAIL: lectorpublishing@gmail.com

9 789353 425463